CELIA'S CHOICE

A Story About Leaving Behind

All That We Hold Dear

Dear Sophia,
Hope you love
the Story!
All the Best,
Nitsa

Nitsa Olivadoti

"You are free to choose, but you are not free from the consequence of your choice."

– A Universal Paradox

This book is a work of fiction. Names, characters, places and incidents either are products of the author's imagination or are used fictitiously. Any resemblance to actual events, locales or persons, living or dead, is entirely coincidental.

Copyright © 2012 by Nitsa Olivadoti

All rights reserved, no part of this publication may be reproduced in whole or in part in any form without prior written permission of the author, except for brief quotes used in connection with reviews.

Edited by Elaina Schlumper

Designed by Nitsa Olivadoti

www.thecicadaseries.com

cicadaseries@gmail.com

TABLE OF CONTENTS

A CICADA'S CONCEPTION.........1

A CICADA'S CHILDHOOD..........65

THE LOCUSTS DESCEND...........116

THE LOCUSTS DEPART.............135

A CICADA'S VULNERABILITY....180

A CICADA'S ADULT LIFE...........208

A CICADA'S SONG...................229

GREEK WORD GLOSSARY..........260

ELENI'S FAMILY TREE..............262

Dedication

This book is dedicated to my family – immediate and extended, in hopes that future generations will read this and feel the essence of their Greek ancestors in their blood. It is my hope that they will too, be inspired to take the journey of educating themselves on this beautiful and ancient place. Perhaps one day they just might set foot on the same stairs where their great-great-great grandmother stood, or observe the magic of a full moon above the Acropolis one warm summer night.

It is the cicada which reminds me of my Yiayia, my grandmother, who I admire endlessly for singing beautiful songs throughout the worst of times. This is the first book in a series of novels that were inspired by her life. She once told me:

"My life is not one amazing love story, but at every turn I have been blessed with amazing love."

Through learning her life story, I have realized that her life journey has been two-fold: First, sing through the hard parts and second, leave the lyrics to your song behind.

Bestowing your experiences and wisdom to your children and their children is the greatest song of all. Thank you, Yiayia, for all of your beautiful stories. They have inspired me endlessly.

Prologue

For over two years I placed my mind and heart between two worlds. There is my reality, where I am the mother to two beautiful children and a wife to a supportive and loving husband. Then, there is my imaginary world where I have been living in Greece through my grandmother's stories. Writing this book at times became an obsession. My mind was occupied with thoughts, sights and conversations my distant relatives may or may not have actually had. Sometimes I felt as if I could hear their voices directly speaking to me, urging me to write, giving me the strength I needed after long days with the children, responsibilities and commitments. When the children were finally were asleep, I began my work day which often lasted into the wee hours of the morning. Days when I was too tired to write, my internal clock never failed to wake me at 3:00 a.m. What was it about 3:00 a.m., I often wondered? I would wake from either a burst of energy or a prophetic-like dream, sometimes both. I was driven to my desk like a madwoman in the middle of the night. My husband did not understand why I could not get up each morning and write from 6:00 to 8:00 a.m. on a schedule. He is an engineer, and everything has an equation in his mind. "Creativity cannot happen like that," I explained. I think back to my college days. My most influential professor told me that if we are lucky, we will notice a time will come when a window opens for us. If we don't go in to find out what is inside, it will close and we may never see it again. This is the story that has lived in me since I was nine years old. I remember following my Yiayia around her kitchen as she cooked delicious food and listened to her Greek music radio station. Many times, she would stop suddenly, snap her fingers, grab my hand and lead me in dances around her table. I asked her to tell me the story of her life, over and over, because I wanted to know everything. I realized three years ago it was time to formally interview her so that I would be able to tell her stories, otherwise I would have to forever hold my tongue (or pen).

As I became enthralled with the stories of love and war, I focused on the difficult choices people made during this time period. Besides the characters themselves, my other obsession was the question of choice. Why we make the choices we do, and the million different scenarios that would have happened or never would have happened because of them. Surely, it caused me to analyze my own life and led me to wonder:

"In the end, do we all have a predetermined fate or are there things we can do to change the outcome?" As you can see, a person stewing on this philosophical idea for too long can drive himself or herself to madness.

This journey is personal to me. I want to leave something behind for my kids and theirs that they will not forget. I want them to love Greece as much as I do, and to learn something about a place and a people that I love with all of my heart. Above all, my goal has been to record the essence of my grandmother's life. These stories are inspired by her, but expanded and romanticized from my own imagination and life experiences. I find so much joy in knowing I am leaving my children and theirs something special, a taste of their roots (no matter how diluted the Greek is by then). I do not want my grandmother's struggles or the hardships of her homeland to ever be forgotten.

A Cicada's Conception

A female cicada lays her eggs deep in the strongest tree branch. The mother, having left her legacy, dies once she knows her children are safe in the world. Humans are more complex. Does a mother's worry or love for her children ever stop? I do not think so.

Voyage (1950)

I turn my eyes to the ocean. I am entranced by the green of the water which coordinates with my seasick skin and hazel eyes. My hair, light and blonde, is unusual for a Greek girl. Fitting, I think, since my life is anything but usual. My thoughts are scattered, that is nothing new, especially since this painful leaving. I am caught up in a stream of endless thoughts and emotions; I hardly know what to think or feel first. As the boat pulled out of the port, its engines roared so loud that my screams could not reach her. They were desperate screams from which my throat still burns. How I wanted, in that moment, to jump into the ocean to reclaim my old life. How I wished I could swim back to my beloved Greece, back into the arms of my mother, home to see the face of the boy who admired me more than anyone I had ever known. If only I could swim. It is too late to learn how now, just like it is too late to finish a sweet and innocent kiss. All that I once had is gone.

Anxiety plagues me, as the memory of Nazi bombs and air raid sirens comes to mind. I was eight years old then, and my country was at war. I recall German planes flying low and shaking the earth with such force, my bones rattled. One day, when I was playing hopscotch outside, a plane came so close, I felt as if I could touch the swastika. As if that wasn't close enough, it made another pass and flew directly over my head. My body froze with fear under the wind and noise of the plane. Warm pee rushed down my legs as I lost control. I remember turning my head toward my mother's voice.

"Eleni!" she screamed, running to me with open arms. It seemed like she moved slowly, as she made her way to where I stood. I had one foot on each square of the hopscotch game, frozen, unable to move. The same feeling consumes me now, raw fear. I remember looking down at the puddle at my feet then up at my mother who took me into her arms as I burst into tears. I can still hear the clink of the flat stones hit the ground as they fell from my hand.

Memories return to reality. I am sixteen years old, married to a complete stranger who waits for me in America. As I make my way across the ocean, I know I have to move forward, but I cannot stop looking back. I stare at home until it dissolves into the salty water, vanishing from the horizon, thinking many thoughts. Like how I always understood that when a woman got married, it was expected her last name was replaced with her husband's. That had always been a natural, expected thing. I could never have foreseen that I would lose my first name, too. My name is Eleni. My husband insisted I get used to the fact I will be called Helen, the English translation, as soon as I stepped foot in America. I admit to being puzzled at first. Why wouldn't I keep my name? It is a beautiful one. I know Helen is the translation of Eleni but it seems like the name is not mine at all. I try to put the strangeness I feel out of my mind, and do what I think is expected of a good wife.

"Helen. Helen." I repeat under my lips as I gaze across the ocean. The two syllables roll off my tongue in an unnatural way. The name feels like it belongs to another. I repeat it again. *"Helen."* If I keep practicing I might get used to it. It was Helen of Troy who was famous for wearing the face that launched a

thousand ships. Helen was the trophy wife of
King Menelaus of Sparta. She lived in an
unhappy marriage to him and longed for true
love. She found it with another, Paris of Troy,
and ran away with him to his kingdom. To get
Helen back, King Menelaus launched a war
that lasted for ten years. In the tenth year of
the war, Menelaus had given up the fight for
his wife. He presented a gift to Troy, a token
of surrender. Menelaus' army had constructed
a large wooden horse and the Trojans opened
their gates to receive it. Once they brought the
horse inside, however, soldiers poured out,
defeating their city. It's hard to believe one
woman created such conflict. I wonder in all
of human history who has gone the furthest,
sacrificed the most, for an earthly love? What
is the difference between love and possession,
passion and reality? Did Helen of Troy feel
something more for her husband after he
fought for her? Or was she still devoid of love,
head hung low in defeat as she reluctantly
went back to him?

As I sail on this ship named *Ellas*
(Greece), the only thing visible for miles is
ocean. Waves crash alongside the ship as it
cuts through the water like a well sharpened
knife. Engines roar as we pick up speed. I love
my country more than words or emotions can
express. I have never been away before from

my beautiful city, *Athina* (Athens). In this ancient land a unique rhythm of life exists. Old, yet new at the same time, it is inspired constantly by the typical Greek mind's thirst for learning and for creating new thoughts and philosophies. This is the inherent character of Greeks from ancient to modern times. Maybe that explains why I am always full of crazy ideas. Like this one, to leave.

In the dramatic landscapes of my country, there are many contrasts. There is the sea, mountains, lush green forests, desert and earth made of red clay. Crumbling ruins lay strewn about; old dedications to the pagan gods which lay beside early Orthodox Christian churches in the Byzantine style. In ancient Greece, the Gods, nymphs and muses frolicked among the temples which now are now no more than scattered stones. I smile when I imagine them with golden hair and white flowing robes. Immortal beauty and perfection. I wonder what it would have been like to live in that time. In one Greek myth, a man named Tithonus, a singer, was granted immortality by Zeus. His lover, Eos, the Goddess of the dawn, had asked Zeus to make him immortal but forgot to ask for eternal youth. The man grew old and small until he turned into a cicada. He buzzed about, begging for death to come for eternity. Even ancient Gods were not immune to ruining love.

Modern Christianity sprung up alongside the pagan gods, and soon Zeus and the other gods who lived on Mount Olympus became myths, leaving behind nothing more than interesting stories. Myths, however do teach us an important lesson; mortal or immortal, we are all imperfect.

O Theos (God)

Orthodox Christian churches are formed in the shape of a cross with a large dome in the center. On the inside, the walls and ceilings are plastered with ornate *icons* – religious images each telling a story about an event or saint that is important in the church's history. I learned in school that religious icons began in a time when most people were illiterate. Each icon depicts a scene that tells a biblical story and shows us important saints. Icons function as windows to heaven in which we glimpse a look into the spiritual world. They are filled with symbolism, and the monks who create them in their monasteries have a complex job. They must fast and pray before, during and after painting them with a pure heart. They also must possess the complicated artistic skill of painting with egg tempera. Most common is The Virgin Mary with baby, Jesus, the ultimate symbol of love and sacrifice. Thinking about it reminds me of my own mother, arms closed in around me tight, eyes filled with purity and love for me, her only child. Behind my mother's encouraging eyes lies the pain of letting me go, the agony of giving part of her own flesh away.

Alone in an unforgiving and difficult world, Mary gave her only child unconditional love and supported his decisions, no matter how hard it was. Her baby, Jesus, would change the world. If she did not let him and held him too tight would he not have had the chance or courage?

Sight is the easiest way to learn, that is why icons have survived for thousands of years. When you see something, touch it, breathe it in, you never forget. Words are fleeting, and even the most well written books will be forgotten eventually. But you never forget the face of your first real love, your first experience of loss. Moments of intense emotion have a way of imprinting on the mind like photographs, they have a certain permanency within the soul. There are certain things we can never forget, like the face of a tear-streaked boy who told you he loved you and you still turned him away. Worst of all, perhaps you loved him too, but did not know it yet.

I wonder about the saints and their personal stories of persecution. Some I know by heart, others I can't remember. I wonder how they had the courage to give up life as they knew it for the promise of something greater, without having material evidence of its existence. I am not built for such bravery, and do not know if I have such faith. My mother does, though. She is so strong. I remember the way she stood tall and confident in the midst of enemy soldiers. She walked beside the Italians and Germans with me, never showing fear or weakness. She calmly took her place among them on the train, as if that is exactly where she belonged. She went back and forth to the city, to bring food to our friends and relatives there when they were starving. She knew the dangers, but it was the right thing to do. She had faith that God would protect us. I stand here today because she was right.

Saints, my mother and my country are the martyrs I know. My own patron saint is said to have found the true cross on which Jesus was crucified in Jerusalem. The story says Saint Eleni knew where to dig for it because a patch of sweet basil grew at the site. Basil became a sacred tool in the church for the dispersal of holy water. The priest dips a bunch of basil in the water and shakes it, blessing the church and its people.

For many centuries Greece has been occupied, at war or persecuted for one reason or another. My country is poor and beautiful, yet ever strong. It is the place that formed our modern civilization. It created and perfected things such as: art, math, science, philosophy and government. When I was a little girl, my father would take me on his lap and explain how the Greeks invented everything, how I should always be proud to be Greek. Even though I heard his speech a thousand times, I liked when he held me near, the sound of his voice and smell of his pipe.

Greece. The place my heart is, where it shall always be. Where your heart resides will always be home, no matter where you are born, live or die. My love of this place runs deep, deeper and more passionate than perhaps what is rational. But to me, everything I feel is rational. Passion might be the only tangible thing I have ever possessed completely in my life. The passion I felt dancing with my arms outstretched, fingers snapping and the blood in my veins that pulsed to the music is an addictive and necessary part of my life. I do not think I have ever been in love with a person, but I am in love with my country.

I swallow hard once again, riddled with acute pangs of anxiety. I pray this is not my last glimpse of home. A whisper escapes my lips as I think my thoughts out loud without notice. *"I miss you..."*

In a trance-like state I pick my lips, a nasty habit that seems to present itself whenever I am nervous. I draw blood as an ample piece of skin has been removed, causing a deep cut. *Why do I do this?* I ask myself, aggravated at my weakness. It has been a struggle of mine since I can remember. Even after my mother's repeated warnings that I would ruin the lips God gave me, I could never quit. I lick the blood away as the taste of salty iron infiltrates my senses.

I feel faint, dizzy and can hardly breathe. The ocean breeze is strong in my face, but the forced oxygen does not help. I feel as if there is a noose around my neck and I am slowly being strangled. I try and stop my slow and painful imagined death and concentrate on breathing.

"In through the nose, out through the mouth," I hear my mother's advice in my head. An odd and pained sound escapes from my lips. It startles me, and my ears do not comprehend the voice is mine.

There is a woman nearby who reminds me of my mother. She is dressed simply in black, a bun in her hair. Deep crevasses cover her leathered skin from many years of exposure to the Aegean sun. Her eyes are a rare shade of blue. I cannot help but stare. I pretend for a moment that it is her and she is with me. I wish it were so. She eyes me with concern.

Emotional pain has taken on a life of its own. Like a dangerous animal gnawing at my body with razor sharp teeth, I am torn inside and out. My sadness is so deep that it begins to manifest physical symptoms. *Will I be alright?* My legs feel as mushy as apricot marmalade. My anxiety has made everything unstable, uneven and weak. My energy is depleted. It won't take long for complete exhaustion to set in.

It kills me to think of my mother hurting like this. We are separate yet sharing these same feelings in these same moments; *I can feel it.* I try my best not to think about her current state but it is all-consuming. Weakness, like an illness, overpowers me, causing my legs to become unstable. I grip the railing of the ship so hard my knuckles turn white like sea foam.

In two weeks I will arrive in America and I will call it home. I ignore the glances strangers give me as I look over the rail and stare into the ocean. I know that I must look so tense, so desperate for something they cannot even begin to understand, and although I try not to make eye contact with the woman who looks like my mother, she is still concerned and lurks nearby. I know that I am, as usual, wearing my heart on the outside. My emotions remain undisguised.

A thick cloud of sadness surrounds me, as the initial excitement and happiness I felt about leaving home begins to fade. Back and forth I dance on the edge of sanity. It is not the type of dancing with arms outstretched, spinning in circles, snapping my fingers, singing like a *tzitzika*. I am rather, on a tightrope dancing, with an endless blackness underneath me. If I fall, If I lose myself, I will be falling forever, never to land, never to recover.

One moment I am happy, the next I am guilt-ridden and depressed. I am only a number among thousands, almost completely lost in the crowd. The only reminder that this is real is the racing of my heart and ticket stub in my hand. I wonder: if I jumped over the edge would anyone see me? Would anyone ever hear my struggle over the engine and waves? Would anyone try to save me or would I fall deeper and deeper into the depths of complete darkness? *Don't fall off the tightrope,* I remind myself.

I never could have imagined it would be me he wanted; that after our brief meeting he would want to marry me. This endearing stranger held the key to everything I thought I would ever want in life. In exchange for this life, I would leave behind my homeland, my mother, my family and friends forever.

Despite my sadness, the sweetness of victory fills me. I am one of the few, the lucky ones to take this road of adventure. After a period of war, my country has a lot of rebuilding to do. The bitterness of the salty sea air reminds me that my decision is bittersweet. It is both selfish and self-less. I have sacrificed the part of myself that has always hoped for true love; I must let go of that piece of myself now. *I can do this,* I remind myself. Hard work and commitment first, then reward will come. *Love. I will learn to love him and I will make him love me.* Riding on my shoulders is a strong sense of responsibility. I can only hope this new future will be worth my pain. I hope I will make all of my friends and family back home proud. My relatives wait anxiously on the other side of the ocean to hear the stories about my new life. They will look for my letters, telling them how leaving Greece has changed my life, how America is even better than I thought it would be. The magnitude of leaving is so heavy, it feels as if my chest is filled with lead. I can almost smell the burn of hot molten metal solidifying around my heart. In my mouth, the bitter metallic taste of leaving overpowers me.

My thoughts are at home with my mother. My sweet, poor, broken-hearted mother. She agreed to let me go. The war left us poor and without my *Papa* and she wanted the best for me. She knew that my father would have wanted this for me, too.

Before I left, as she helped me pack my things, she periodically stopped to clutch her chest, breathing deep with her eyes closed tight. I pretended not to notice, but the pain radiated to my own heart simultaneously. Our connection is so intense, sometimes I feel like we share the same soul.

At the end of the summer, a *xenos* (foreigner) arrived. This red-haired foreigner was Greek, but he was not born in Greece. He came from America to marry a young woman and take her home. At first, he had not planned to marry me. Another girl had been arranged for him by his parents. How terrible she must have felt when he no longer wanted to marry her, when her dream of living in America dissolved before her. This *xenos* decided to take me for his wife. His name, is George.

Unconditional

I take a deep breath of salty sea air as my thoughts float back to my mother. Every thought I have leads back to her. Vasiliki is her name, which I always found fitting because *vasiliko* (sweet basil) is her most treasured herb and scent on earth. The smell of basil comforts me, as if it is an extension of her. I feel for the leaves of basil in my pocket, which I had plucked from her garden before I left. They are dry now, and crumble as I touch them. I am afraid they will turn to dust and blow from my hand into the ocean if I take them out, so I decide to keep them safe inside.

My mother is beautiful. Her skin is porcelain, without a single blemish or wrinkle. She had me later in life and was well in to her thirties, old not only in her time, but still by today's standards. From what I understand, pregnancy did not come easy for her, and even when she did get pregnant no babies clung to her womb aside from me. I am her only child.

My mother's eyes are bluer than the bluest sky and her hair is warm and brown like roasted chestnuts. *How I loved the smell of my mother cooking chestnuts over an open fire.* *Kastana* (chestnuts) are dry, juicy, warm, sweet, nutty and pasty all at the same time. I loved the cool fall nights when my family would sit together and eat their warm goodness, talking, laughing and telling stories.

My mother's hair was always swept up in a neat bun. I don't remember her ever cutting it. The only time I ever saw it flow in long waves that reached past her belly was after she washed it. I would sit on the edge of her bed, admiring her as she brushed it. I could have sat there for hours, watching. But she did not fuss over herself, so it did not take her long.

My mother's physical strength is phenomenal. She does everything in the house, even the jobs that were usually designated for men. She is tough. She was raised in the village. She came into marriage knowing more about fixing things in our home than my father did. My father was a businessman, who had to have his pants and shirts pressed just so and his shoes shined every day. I remember my mother doing that for him. My mother wore simple house dresses and she never shined her shoes. They were always a little dusty from the garden and she liked them that way.

Although her physical strength is admirable, it is no match for her gifts of intuition and compassion. Her instincts and genuine care and love for others emanate from her. The sort of love she exudes is unconditional and it is not only reserved for her family. She feels everyone is connected in this world. It is not just about blood. She believes all souls are tied together by invisible strings. If one hurts, we all do. Not everyone sees the world this way.

Her heart breaks for her country in the aftermath of Greece's wars. There were three: the Italian war, the German war and our own civil war between the right and left leaning citizens. This last war was the greatest tragedy of all. After all the country had been through, fathers, sons and brothers fought each other over various political views on governing the post-war era of our country. We became broken people, who had forgotten we should have worked together to solve our problems, and my country and its people suffered greatly.

In the aftermath of these wars, people roamed the streets mourning their losses. Some shuffled along like they were barely alive, mumbling words of madness, sadness and regret. I can never forget the things I saw. Images were burned into my young eyes that I will never forget. War is not fair. It is not a solution. How can it possibly be? Humans always find their way back to the senseless violence, as if killing has ever caused a positive change anywhere in this world.

I pray a lot about the world. I have prayed to God to somehow bestow on us simultaneous enlightenment; elevate all to a higher state of consciousness. However, in my short sixteen years of life I have already come to the realization that you cannot change people and the patterns to which they have committed, and it is through mistakes and tragedies that humans learn and evolve. I think the human condition is much like the instinct of a wild animal. You can tame them, break them and try your best to change them. However, underneath, their true nature will come to the surface at some point. There is no permanent switch, no disconnecting any of us from who we truly are. All it takes is the right moment, the right place. There will always be conflict.

Humanity is the subject I studied most during the years of war. When the schools were closed, my mother taught me what she could with the tools she had available. She taught me about God, people, love and sacrifice. My life experience during this period became my education. My mother and I escaped soldiers and bombs, gave to those who needed it, and learned to make the best of any situation. I might not be able to solve math equations or repeat facts from my old history books, but I know what it means to survive. I know what it means to lose. I know what it means to love.

My mother was born in a small village called Klitora, which lies in the Peloponnesus region, a mountainous place located in Southern Greece. From Athens, the trip took hours by train. My mother said when she was a child they had to take a donkey.

"You are very lucky, Eleni. When I was a kid it took days," she would often remind me. I rolled my eyes sometimes because I was tired of hearing it.

High up in my mother's mountains, the air is clean, thin and blue. There is a certain flavor in the atmosphere, which I can only describe as crunchy and delicious. My mother's *horyo* (village) is where we would go every year with my cousins in the summer. When the city got too congested with unbearable heat, we needed to escape. The atmosphere that surrounded us high in the cool mountains can be summed up in one word: simple. I realize why my mother's need for material things fell very low on her list of priorities when I think of her *horyo*. She never became the type of Athenian woman who followed the latest fashion trends. She detests getting herself into a dress and putting on make-up. She would much rather be in her garden among fresh herbs, tomatoes and cucumbers. Basil grew around her feet like weeds. It was as if she and the herb had an understanding. She would love it, and it would grow for her. She would pick it by the handful, face glowing with pride, as she inhaled its unique scent. After working in her garden all day, her knee-high socks ended up rolling down below her dress hem. She just laughed. Her unpainted nails were short with traces of garden soil underneath. My mother did not care. She loved her garden. From her vegetable harvest, nothing was wasted. This was an important lesson she learned from living through tough times as a child. Whatever could not be eaten was jarred or dried. She hid away money in various places, prepared for any situation. My mother wanted to make sure we could survive anything.

My mother does not judge, so I never heard her say the words I am thinking right now about my own decision: *I am selfish for wanting more when I have everything I need.* She must not understand what more I could want. But she will never utter those words because she loves me unconditionally. She wants me to learn about life on my own terms and I love and respect her even more for it. I had all I ever needed in Greece: love, food and family. I appreciate my life and my mother more than she will ever know. She always told me it was important to "love with your heart, not with things."

To her, nothing else mattered as long as we had love and good health. I knew that she was right. But I am not as wise and patient as my mother. Being grateful for everything and never wanting more for the rest of my life is unfathomable to me. I am curious. I don't have the self-control not to want beautiful things that I don't need or the strength to stop fantasizing about places I have never been. I cannot stop thinking about the things I have never done that I long to do. Sometimes I wish I could be more like her and I wonder: *When will I become fully satisfied?*

Getting settled so that I can find a way to get my mother to the United States will be my first priority in America. My heart aches for the moment of our reunion.

Last Glance

Anxiety continues to plague me. The image of the way my mother looked as the ship departed will be my last memory of her for whatever length of time we will be apart. She was so brave in saying good-bye, I thought it was strange. I knew my mother and could feel her holding back the flood of emotions for my benefit. I am all she has in this world. Despite her efforts, I witnessed the break-down she had been trying so hard not to let me see.

After I entered the ship, I hurriedly made my way to the edge of the nearest deck – to the left side where I knew she was standing with my *Theo* (Uncle) Stathis. I wedged myself in between the crowd of people waving to loved ones with white handkerchiefs.

They were the same white cotton cloths we twirled in circles when dancing. I would always try to get in the lead as my body pulsed to the rhythmic beat. Of course, I was always singing. Everyone held hands, and wove in and out of each other, between tables and chairs, singing the most beautiful words about love, heartbreak and the country we loved so much. I remember my mother and father dancing in the kitchen to one song in particular:

"We are poor but at least we can watch the stars together… our roof is leaking, our hearts breaking and we are so poor but we love each other… so you and I and this little house is all we need… with our little ones sleeping near and the scent of basil blowing in our window…"

The depth always moved me. Music made me sad, happy, excited, anxious and full of admiration all at once. I am Greek. Drama, love, heartache, my country and God are ingrained in my being. Though I am leaving, Greece will never leave me. It is impossible to separate Greece from your heart once you have fallen in love with it. Some of the greatest writers, poets and philosophers have said so. I have heard this explanation of the Greek soul and I believe it is true:

"The most painful experience a Greek can know: to be an orphan, to be alone, to be in love and to be far away from Greece. To be far away from Greece is the worst of all."

As people on the ship wave their handkerchiefs, the mood is somber and nothing like a festive celebration. People cry as they call out to the ones they love. I think it is funny how everything has an opposite, even these small pieces of cloth we hold in our hands. As the handkerchiefs take on the opposite role of joy, to collectors of tears and sorrow, the ship prepares to depart. The anchors are lifted. I pull out my handkerchief and wave it as hard as I can. It looks like a white flag, surrendering. *My surrender*.

It took some time to locate my mother and *theo* (uncle) as I scanned the crowd.

Finally, I saw them. I waved at them both excitedly, jumping up and down. But suddenly, I froze. Like a frightened deer I could not move a bone in my body, my eyes locked on the horrific scene below. I became paralyzed. My mother and *theo* were not waving, laughing or crying. My mother was struggling to stand. She threw one of her arms around his shoulder. He held the hand she draped over his shoulder with one hand and with the other he supported her at the waist. Her feet dangled a few inches from the ground. Her head hung low as she shook it back and forth. I shuttered as chills ran up my spine. This image of her burned my eyes. It was too painful. Her body collapsed in anguish and my heart broke into a thousand pieces. Seeing her like that was the moment that unglued me completely. I felt sickened from the pain of our separation. I became horrified with my decision three weeks too late. I started to scream: "*Mama* (mom)! *Manoula-mou* (my mother)! Over here! I love you, I love you...please... over here! Please! Look up!"

I did not know if she heard me calling, she did not look up. My *theo* helped her rest on a large rock and she buried her face in her hands. *He* stood with his hand on her shoulder and looked up at the ship. He waved towards it, but I could tell he did not see me. *"Theo! Theo!"* I cried.

He took a seat next to my mother. I panicked. My breathing grew fast and heavy, my heart ready to come out of my chest. I tried once more to call to her as loud as I could, but the ship turned on its propellers, drowning out my voice. We started to move.

"Mama! Mama!"

Soon the ship was out of the harbor. My mother and my *theo* soon looked like tiny specks on my homeland. I stood on the deck, stunned. My handkerchief fell from my hand into the ocean.

Back to the Present

I make myself relive that horrific scene over and over. I cannot stop myself from seeing it; my mother's collapse. The last glimpse I had of her makes my heart sink. Around my heart, an invisible fist is squeezing it tighter and tighter with every beat. I am anxious, alone, and I feel like I might die. There is no one to catch me if my legs get weak and I faint. I must be brave. *Compose yourself Eleni*, I tell myself. The wind whips my hair. *Good-bye Manoula. Good-bye my Greece.* I cry.

For the last three weeks, I have lived in a dream. It was a nice dream, this fairy tale in which I lived. I was happy, weightless, curious and excited. But today, I finally woke up. It feels like a bucket of ice water has been thrown at me, leaving me shocked and gasping in surprise, because reality is hard and at times shocking but fantasies are wonderful and euphoric. I am not living in a fairy tale anymore. I flinch and shudder. I am wide awake. The truth is, it was my choice to leave, mine alone.

I wish my mother did not always want for me what I wanted. If so, I would not be going away from her. She would not have pressured me if I said no to George's proposal, but she did not try and change my mind when I said yes. I look toward home as the sea widens between us. A warm, salty breeze tickles my nose and dries my tears.

I have heard the Atlantic is not as pretty, blue or warm as the ocean in Greece. I will miss my ocean. I will miss the feeling of family, warmth and sunshine. I will miss the smell of sweet jasmine and gardenia blooming on warm summer nights when soft breezes carry their perfume. I will miss the persistent humming of the cicadas in the tree tops. My constant singing had brought my nickname *Tzitzika* (Cicada) to life. I wonder about my new family in America. *Will they understand me and like me? Will they be nice to me? Will they be as serious as my husband?* Worry consumes me. In Greece, everyone I knew was so vibrant. Life may not have always been easy, but it was fun and full of love. Even during the war, my life was beautiful.

The late fall weather started to settle in before I left. I heard that in New England it is very cold and that winter has begun. In my mind, I am ready for summer, not snow. I know that it will not be for many months, but I can hardly wait. I have already decided I will not like winter in my new home, but I will survive it. Cold weather and cold people have never agreed with me. I belong to the summer. But I will be brave, like my mother until the warm days come back around. For the cicada, winter means death. I relate to the cicada's pain, as I sail into a cold sea, because part of me is dying as well.

I wonder if I will find my favorite fruit in America. Sika (figs) have a certain color and flavor unlike any other. Red. Warm. Hearth. Home. I taste them in my mind and recall how I loved to peel back their soft skin to reveal their sweetness inside. I remember the *yifties* (gypsies) as they rode their bicycles with baskets filled with the gorgeous fruit, shouting: "*Sika! Sika!*" I would beg my mother for a coin and run after the peddlers, buying as many as I could carry. Sometimes I felt sick from my selfish binges, but it was worth it.

I think of the olive groves and vast wheat fields where I went running all summer long in my mother's *horyo*. I would play for hours, laughing with my cousins. My three boy cousins were the sons of my *Theo* Stathis and *Thea* (Aunt) Maritsa and they were like my own brothers; Adonis, Yiorgos and Vangeli. My cousins, along with every person I love, I will carry with me. *I will come back to them one day*; I make this promise to myself.

My Boys

Last night I had to say my final good-byes. "No... No! You can't go!" Vangeli cried. I hugged him tight and caressed his messy hair. I treated him like he was my own baby since he was born back in 1940, when my country was on the verge of the Greek-Italian war. He is eight years old now, one year older than I was when the first war began. He is short, round and sloppy. When he was a toddler, I would constantly tuck in his shirts and wash his muddy hands and shoes. I was not asked to do this, it was my own desire to mother him. I had no siblings of my own. I liked to comb his hair and wash his face. I would take his shoes, wash his laces separately then shine them. Usually only minutes after I cleaned him, he was covered with mud. My *thea* thanked me, but warned me many times it was simply not worth it. Sometimes I ran after him, threatening to beat his bottom just like his mother did when he wrecked his Sunday clothes before church. The night before I departed for America was filled with all kinds of emotions and memories.

My mother took an icon from the wall and packed it in many layers of cloth for protection. It was an icon of Mary holding baby Jesus. She kissed before she laid it in the trunk.

The attachment I have with my cousins runs deep and parting from them is more difficult than I could have imagined. I have no siblings of my own, but if I did, I imagine they would be just like Adonis, Vangeli, and Yiorgos. A part of my heart has been ripped out permanently in leaving them.

Adonis is the oldest at seventeen, ten months older than me, strong-minded, mischievous and comical. He often looked for and found trouble, and enjoyed dragging me into it. I will miss him. Most of the time I was not afraid and up for any challenge he presented, (at least not until my mother caught wind of it and ran after my bottom with a stick or a spoon). He was strikingly handsome. Once we entered our teenage years, dreamy-eyed girls swarmed around him, competing for his attention. Sometimes I couldn't help but feel protective. (No girl will ever be good enough for my cousin.) Yiorgos, the middle child, is twelve. Thin and whiny, he was the one to tattle on me and Adonis. We dreaded his high-pitched voice calling for our mothers when we had done something fresh, such as playing a practical joke, sneaking out of the house or skipping school. My mother and *Thea* Maritsa were tough women and did not tolerate misbehavior in any form. We got many beatings because of Yiorgos.

"My bags are all packed. I think I am ready," I told Adonis, biting my bottom lip.

"*Tzitzika...*" he said. Tears welled up in my eyes at the sound of my special name. The name nobody would know in America. In America, apart from my husbands' family, they wouldn't even call me by my real name, Eleni. They would never know that my family, friends and neighbors nicknamed me *Tzitzika* because I was always buzzing around and singing. I knew I would have to behave like a grown lady, a wife from that point forward. So, I decided to do my best to tuck away every childish thing. I thought to myself: As soon as the ship docks I will be called Helen. I will miss both of my identities – my birth name Eleni and my nickname *Tzitzika*. The old me will recede like the tide... it will disappear.

"I promise I will visit you in America one day," Adonis said.

Just then Yiorgos came into the kitchen. "Hey *Tzitzika* - don't run away again, alright?" he said, slapping my shoulder and laughing. The memory of my wedding night came flooding back. I frowned and felt my cheeks grow hot.

"I am joking, Eleni. Please don't be mad with me!" I gave him a dirty look but I could not help but laugh.

"Why? Are you going to tell on me?" I asked, smirking.

Yiorgos was most interested in America for himself. I think he was jealous and fascinated simultaneously.

"Listen, you have to write me and tell me about the snowstorms you get. I heard where you are going to live you get snow up to your chest! If it is really true, you have to tell me everything, and send photographs!"

Goosebumps formed when I thought about winter and I involuntarily shivered. "I promise," I told him.

Adonis joked: "*Tzitzika*... I hope you don't get punished too much with children as terrible as us. Actually... I hope you do," he said, nudging me with his elbow as he winked one eye. After we laughed, there was an uncomfortable silence.

Adonis had tears in his eyes, which brought me to the verge of falling apart. The four of us stood together and joined hands in a secret handshake which we had created and shared since we were little. We put our hands together in the middle of a circle and counted:

"*Ena, thio, tria* (one, two, three)!" and raised our hands up. We all laughed, cried and hugged. *Thea* Maritsa and *Theo* Stathis looked on adoringly. I turned to my *thea* and hugged her for a long time.

"Come back as soon as you can, please?"

"I will, *Thea*. I promise," I said.

I turned to my *Theo* Stathis and he said, "See you tomorrow morning, Eleni. I am going to take you and your mother to the port with my truck. I hope there is enough room in there for all of your things; you have a lot for a little girl."

I smiled.

"I'll be knocking on your door early, so get some sleep," he said.

"Thank you, *Theo*," I said, hugging him tight. I took one last look at all of them. I inhaled deeply and left.

Eleni & Thanasi

It was getting dark, but I had to see my other cousins, Eleni and Thanasi again. *Thea* Maria and *Theo* Panayotis are their parents. *Theo* Panayotis is my father's brother.

My cousin Eleni could not hide her doubt. She was the only person who openly displayed concern about George's personality. In the short courtship we had, she saw him more than anyone else. She came on almost every date with us, yet she could not put her finger on the cause of her uneasiness

"Can you delay the marriage?" Eleni would ask. I rolled my eyes. How could she ask such a thing? Would a few more weeks even matter? George had a good job; he had already gone back to America to his work. Time was not a luxury I had. Eleni was frustrated with the fact she only had a few weeks to figure George out, and she never could.

When I entered the house, Eleni looked distraught. Sometimes I wondered whether she had become another victim of jealousy. But deep inside, I knew the truth. She did not want to see me go. She was afraid for me. I did not want to leave her, either.

"Eleni, Thanasi!" I opened my arms to them.

Eleni is fourteen, a little younger than me. Her fair skin coupled with curly red hair is striking. It has the same exact color and curl as her mother's, my *Thea* Maria. *Thea* Maria would often make the most wonderful vegetable dishes with sautéed onion, eggplants, tomatoes, kale and fresh feta cheese. Her house always smelled delicious.

Thanasi is eighteen, a few years older than me. Tall, dark and well-spoken like his father. Yianni is his best friend. Thanasi knows the story of us. He knows the pain of his best friend but tried not to intrude on my happiness or judge me. His father made it clear that my father would have wanted this for me. He is more loyal to his own blood than friends. His thoughts were translucent, so I asked:

"Take care of Yianni for me, please?"

My cousin squinted his eyes and crinkled his nose.

"Eleni, don't worry about us here. We will all be fine. You have a new life. Go to it."

What can be said at this point? What did I gain from a request he could not fulfill? Nothing. Eleni looked at me and I knew what to expect from her lips before she said a word.

"Are you sure you want to do this? I mean, it is not too late. You have not gone yet..."

"Eleni!" I exclaimed in an aggravated tone.

"I already ran away once, and I promised I would never do that again to my husband."

I quickly realized I should have been more sensitive. She was my best friend. I put my hand in hers and looked into her eyes: "Please, Eleni. Don't ask me this again. You know it is too late. We are married. I have made my decision. Everything is going to be just fine, you'll see," I assured her.

"Promise me. Whatever you do, be careful. If George doesn't treat you right…. Don't be afraid to… to… I don't know. *Leave*. Him. If you ever have to," she told me.

"Eleni, you worry too much!" I blurted. Her nervous behavior towards me had been typical since the day George made us leave the movies. But I was already married to him and I was leaving the next morning. I wished she would stop her behavior, because I needed her support, not someone who would add to the anxiety I already had.

I had my own uncertainties about George and her worry, her advice made everything harder. I pushed her words aside, tried to change my tone of annoyance and hugged her tight.

"I will write you soon. We will write to each other all of the time," I promised.

I hugged Thanasi, Eleni, *Thea* Maria and *Theo* Panayotis. My *Theo*, who made drinking wine his second full-time job, held my shoulders and said: "Your father would be proud, *Tzitzika*. He always dreamed for his only daughter to have the best life possible. God rest his soul, his dream has come true."

"Thank you, *Theo*," I said, grateful for his encouragement. I took one last look at the beloved faces staring at me and turned for the door. I was losing my resolve in saying good-bye to my family. I needed to get to the comfort of my home and my mother quickly. I took a deep breath as my feet hit the dirt road and I ran. I ran as if I was running for my life, running out of fear, running for my freedom or perhaps all three. Tears blurred my vision but I didn't care, I let them fall without wiping them away. There was one more person I wanted to see, but I was afraid. I ran past his house. The lights were still on. My feet kept on moving, they did not stop. I did not dare let them. I told him how I felt and said good-bye. I would not change my mind. I sprinted through my front door and slammed it behind me. It was done. I needed to spend the last few moments with my mother, the one who mattered most.

Gone

A chill runs up my spine as the ocean breeze picks up with the increasing speed of the ship. I have been so immersed in my thoughts and emotions, more time has passed than I realize. My Greece is gone. There is nothing but the large, empty ocean in front of me. I am so tired of crying, and I am filled with anxiety and anticipation. This long trip will give me plenty of time to try and imagine what my new life will bring.

Leaving my mother was the hardest thing I had ever done. I put on my "strong face," a name I made up for a certain expression I learned from watching her. I was dying inside, though I hid it well when I left her. I did not want to upset her more than she was already, and I wanted her to believe I was completely happy. Sadness stabs my body like knives, plunging deeper with every beat. *What have you done?* I ask myself, forgetting to breathe.

There is no time to second guess things now, I am moving in open water with no escape. There is no going back on the promises I have made. I am married and I have committed to this man in front of God and my family. George went back to America after a few weeks and planned to send for me once my immigration papers were in order. Now I am on my way to him, to claim his names and his life – my new identity. *Helen Pappas.* George told me that Pappas is not his parent's original last name, but that it was cut to Pappas to make the paperwork easier when his parents arrived at Ellis Island, New York fifty years ago. Papanikolaou was Pappas according to the United States government. It seems strange to me, this wonderful free country that places such a high priority on changing names.

Love is a place I have created in my mind. Only in my dreams have I lived there and witnessed what love entailed. Playing marriage with my dolls was my closest experience to the real thing. Romantic songs that I sang to on the radio with my girlfriends thrilled me, but did I really understand what they meant? No. But the lyrics about love gave me hope that one day I would marry a man who loved me as deep as the ocean and I would love him, too. Deep in the pit of my stomach, anxiety grows... I know *nothing* about men, marriage or being a wife. *Nothing*.

My stomach churns like the water underneath. I breathe deeply and try to find calm. Everything will be fine, I must believe it. Forcing my breath to enter slowly through my nose and out through my mouth, I count. Counting when anxious or angry is a lesson I learned from my mother. But the trembling involuntarily returns as soon as I end this practice and the short, panicked breaths return. I cannot conquer my anxiety alone.

"The shallower the breath, shorter the life left," I heard an old village woman say once. *Am I going to die? Can I have a heart attack at sixteen?* The shallow breath theory scares me because I saw it with my own eyes. I remember my father's last breaths how they appeared to be on the surface, not deep in the lungs. That is how I learned the end was close. Death has a specific time, decided for us long before we were born. I do not think we can control it, just like now, I cannot control my racing heart, as it pounds twice as fast and so hard it takes my breath away. If God intends to take me, I know I have no power over it. So, I continue to weather my mind through this maddening storm and pray for relief.

A few short weeks ago, I became a wife. It was my *Theo* Stathis and *Theo* Panayotis who convinced my mother that she should not worry. I was young, but I had learned and seen much from living through war. They decided that I was wise, and strong enough to handle myself. *Theo* Panayotis told my mother that my father would have wanted this. My mother's ability to fulfill a wish of my father's in death gave my mother purpose, and perhaps, a hint of his presence.

"She does have the maturity of at least a twenty year old," *Thea* Maritsa assured my mother. Maybe she is right. I do not think of myself as a child, despite how much I still need my mother. Witnessing danger and death at such a young age has had a profound influence on my life. I remember everything as if it happened yesterday, even though I was only seven when it all began. It was war that took my father. No child should witness what I did. War damaged the child inside of everyone. When the bombs dropped, even the *tzitzikas* fell silent.

Angeliki

The sound of waves crashing permeates my ears. I am happy for the distraction, although it is weak. The ship hums on with no end in sight. Water stretches before me as far my eyes can see. I know somehow, somewhere this empty sea will come to an end, that soon my eyes will be filled with the beauty of the American landscape and the statue of a lady who holds a large torch.

Marrying at sixteen is not uncommon in Greece, but no one I have ever known has married an American and left their family. I am the first to leave, and it is a privilege. Yet, I know I am failing at the unspoken, but expected, most important responsibility as a Greek child: taking care of your parents. I will bring my mother to America to live with me as soon as I can, though I truly am not sure how long it will take.

My mother and my *Thea* Maritsa were convinced envious eyes were upon me once my engagement was made public. My mother attached the *mati,* a pendant of the "evil eye" underneath my skirt with a pin. It is supposed to ward off evil things like jealousy. My mother was convinced I needed to wear it. I reach down and feel it from the outside of my skirt, relieved I remembered to bring it.

My friend Angeliki, with her long straight black hair and hazel eyes was a few years older than me. My mother never approved of our friendship. She was worried older girls could be a bad influence. My mother's intuition proved true when Angeliki became pregnant. She and her boyfriend, Manolis, were forced into immediate marriage. Although it was expected, the poor boy could not help himself from trembling when Angeliki's father burst into his home holding his loaded hunting rifle to his chest. "The decision is simple," he told Manolis. "Marry my daughter or I will shoot you dead, right here, right now."

Church bells soon rang for the young couple. They had a quick, small ceremony and moved in to her mother's house.

"Look, a honeymoon baby!" her mother repeated over and over to anyone who would listen. Folks smiled and turned away, rolling their eyes. There were no secrets in our neighborhood. Angeliki's wedding happened fast, even faster than my own. I remember feeling her warm smile when I told her about my marriage, yet I sensed envy in her eyes. My mother pinned the *mati* to me for Angeliki and all of the others who might have wished they were in my place. Was this worry my mother had necessary? Did Angeliki feel the way I assumed? Or had my ego grown too large for my teenage body? I could speculate, but I would never know. After all, *I* was the one leaving the security and love of home. *I* married a stranger. Angeliki had the boy she had always loved, from the beginning. He was forever hers now. Perhaps having a baby with Manolis and becoming a wife was exactly what she wanted. *Maybe I should be the jealous one.*

I am still not sure what I want. Only that I want something more. I wonder if Angeliki's forced marriage would become dull over time. I hope for her, this is not the case. But my mind wanders and there are so many questions: *What if she thought she loved Manolis because they've grown together, because she knows nothing else? What if one day she has regrets because the marriage was not her choice but her father's?*

Not only was it her father's choice, it is a cultural norm, dictated by the lives and opinions of all of our surrounding family and friends. She did the only thing she could do, not to be shunned. She was pregnant and she had to get married. I am lucky to have had a choice to do something different, something exciting that nobody I have ever known has done before.

Angeliki's life is set; a predictable one with a future much the same as that of her own parents laid out before her, like a map. She will take one road and she knows all of the stops until the end. I take a deep breath, wondering if a simple life would be more comforting. Sailing into uncharted waters alone is certainly not easy.

Yianni

I heard once that sometimes when it comes to love, you can make decisions with your mind that neglect your heart or you can follow your heart and neglect your mind. If your heart and mind are not connected, and you jump into a choice – that is when you make the biggest mistakes.

As I stand alone on the deck of this ship, I cannot stop the constant stream of conflicting thoughts. Then, suddenly and involuntarily, his name escapes my lips. My mother, my family, my homeland – these are not the only reasons for my state. These are not the only people and things I will miss. There is a certain other person nagging at my conscience: *"Yianni."* A barely audible whisper emerges in a voice I do not recognize as my own; again, for the second time in only minutes, a sound flows from my mouth that I cannot control. Almond angelic eyes, so perfect and innocent, haunt me. I hurt this boy and I hate myself for it. Yianni is eighteen, two years older than me. As soon as we became teenagers it was clear he wanted to marry me. We were both young and he was waiting for the right time to ask. Our parents thought we should be a little older. He must regret his patience now.

His parents and two sisters, Vaso and Athena, loved me and thought we were the perfect match. Both of our families seemed to be waiting for the happy day of our marriage. But another plan appeared out of nowhere. My husband, George, tilted my little world off its axis. Marriage had to be executed at what seemed like lightning speed. I had no time to think much or even prepare the logistics. Yianni didn't have much of a chance to absorb what was happening to me. *Did I love him? Does he love me?* Yes. If it didn't stop me from saying yes to George then our love wasn't strong enough. *Right?* I question myself. As usual, there are no answers, only silence.

I denied Yianni's desperate pleas: "Have you lost your mind? Don't do this! Don't leave Greece. What about your mother?" His words still ring fresh in my ears. The guilt of rejecting him and leaving my mother makes my head spin and stomach hurt.

I don't know if I will ever be able to forgive myself. Turning a young and innocent love into a thousand mangled pieces surely deserves some retribution for which I am prepared to endure. Whatever sort of punishment is in store for me, I decide, I am prepared for the fallout.

Lunacy has taken over, even though I know this crying, shaking and sputtering will not serve me. There is a good chance I will never reach my destination. Soon enough I will be locked away on grounds of insanity, I am sure of it. I may never see my husband's face again. *Would that be so bad?* The thought hits me with such surprise, my mouth drops open.

George, my husband, with all of the promise of America, is a good man. I want this new life and the things that will come along with it. I am leaving behind those I love most and have turned away Yianni for this. Have I been a courageous pioneer or a stupid little girl?

I reflect on both men, realizing the striking differences in the lives I would lead with one versus the other. The only similarity they shared was wanting to marry me. I was left to choose and I had to do it quickly. *My choice.* The voice inside of me hisses.

I bring my fingertips to my lips, remembering the first and last time Yianni's were pressed against them. Both of my uncles had been patrolling the neighborhood in an effort to ensure we never had the opportunity to see each other.

"He will take her away and elope with her! Then what? My brother's plans for Eleni will be ruined!" I overheard my *Theo* Panayotis say.

Thea Maritsa murmured something I could not decipher.

"Please, Maritsa, don't add your opinions now!" my *Theo* Stathis snapped. My uncles insisted on protecting me to ensure I got the opportunity to leave not only for me, but to honor my father's dream.

One night, Yianni managed to get past their guard. It was silly of my uncles to think he would whisk me away and carry me to a priest. It was preposterous to think he would do something against my will. Unless, perhaps, it was *me* they did not trust...

Yianni's kiss had been so sweet. I blushed when I thought of how my lips tingled for hours after, especially since I had just gotten engaged. It was wrong; I should not have let it happen. Yet, how I wished I had the courage to kiss him back, to feel more, but why? Why did I want to do this to myself? What is the sense of wondering now? Pressing my fingertips to my mouth, I try to see if some part of him is still with me. This kiss lingers as I continue to dangle my heart over this flame. *Why am I still doing this? I am married.*

On the battlefield which exists in my mind, I struggle. A strange war has erupted within. On opposites sides are excitement and anxiety, ready to fight one another at the smallest threat. Neither side moves; both are frozen, waiting. I cannot decide which side I am on. My feelings change by the minute, by the second. Will these feelings of happiness and sadness simultaneously exist in me indefinitely? How naive to think I can choose a side within one body when in the end, I will only hurt myself.

In America, who will save me from myself? *Will George be there for me? Is he that type of man? Who is he, deep down inside?* These short weeks at sea, I realize, mark only the beginning of my emotional upheaval.

Memories

Happy memories are abundant from every part of my life, and flow through my mind fast and fluid. Even during the war, I was a child and had no realization of the dangers surrounding us. I hugged my beautiful baby doll my parents had gotten me for my birthday before war began. I held her tight in wonder as the first bombs fell. At first I was mesmerized by their beauty, the flashes in the night sky, because they looked and sounded like fireworks.

I remember teetering on a see-saw with my cousin Eleni, both of us laughing hard. She said something hilarious which I cannot remember now, but I almost wet my pants. Her laughing face and mine moving up and down in joy, laughter, and childhood innocence is so clear in my mind. We always loved the fact we shared the same name. Maybe because of our names we felt extra close. The laughter we shared still feels contagious long after our childhood days. I smile. Memories of Eleni bring warmth to my soul. I am so lucky to have her. But as quick as her memory came to me, it disappears. It gets smaller and smaller; hard to see. Then, she is gone. I am unable to recreate it, no matter how I try. I cannot get the moment back. Everyone that I know and love is unreachable. No one can get back moments. I can't even get this moment of remembering back in the same way. Once they are gone, they are gone. What if I try to imagine her in five years and I forget everything? What if my old life fades and becomes a distant memory? I am afraid.

Before I boarded the ship named *Ellas*, my cousin Eleni and I had a professional photographer take some photographs of us.

"What is the special occasion?" he asked.

"My cousin is getting married. She is moving to America," Eleni told him.

The photographer turned to his assistant and told her: "She needs red lipstick. She should look like a married woman, not a child."

The assistant put thick, velvet red on perfectly. It felt sticky and tasted terrible.

"Smile!" The photographer said. Twenty flashes later, we had captured our last moments together.

I wipe another tear from the corner of my eye and try to change focus. Imagining is easy, so I try to picture what America will be like. I look forward to the glamorous lives American women lead. Movie stars, television, pampered housewives, doting husbands, big homes, big cars, endless necessities and wants, coupled with endless opportunities to make money.

I imagine it is a land of beautiful places and people, like California. I have seen photos of it before, palm trees and sunshine. I wonder how far it is from Boston and when we will be able to go. I have heard about the machines Americans watch called a television, a box from which you can view movies, plays and different programs. I am not entirely sure how it works, but I cannot wait to see one for myself. George promised we would buy one together.

Boston, Massachusetts is where I will begin my new life. I am scared now, but it will be good, perhaps better than good. Focusing on the positive takes an enormous amount of effort, but I try. I know what a blessing I have been given. Yianni has to understand this. If he truly loved me, he would want this opportunity for me. Even if it means we will never be together. Life in America will be better for me and my mother.

Leaders

Lost in thought once more, as I drift on the open sea further from home, I see myself as a little girl. My mother had a hiding place in her bedroom closet with coins and a roll of money. She added to it often, saving everything she could little by little. I looked at her, puzzled. I wondered why she had to collect this in secrecy.

"A man does not need to know everything, Eleni," she told me, smiling. She explained it was a secret from my father because this was for emergencies, and that sometimes he was too free with his money. She couldn't wait to see the look on his face whenever we encountered a desperate situation and she came to the rescue. It hadn't happened yet, but she was sure at some point something would arise. She was always a few steps ahead. Clever and intuitive as always, she felt something coming that we didn't. Following the advice of her sixth sense, showcased her *yifti* (gypsy) spirit. All of the women in my family had it, my mother the most. She even hid other things, like dry pasta, rice, candy and preserved goods under her mattress. I thought it was strange, yet it was strange to no one when the war was upon us and we needed them. We were grateful and everyone she shared it with marveled at her cleverness.

Greece entered World War II because Mussolini, the *Duce* (leader) of Italy, and his frustration with Hitler, the *Fuehrer* (leader) of Germany, led him to drag neutral Greece into the war. Mussolini wanted to make Rome a world power. Hitler and Mussolini were colleagues who at first, seemed to have the same motives. But soon, Hitler took Europe by storm, leaving Mussolini in the dust. Mussolini grew frustrated and angry. Both fascist leaders believed in radical measures and ideologies. They wanted to purge people, ethnicity, ideas and current systems to implement their own. To them, violence and war were necessary actions in order to create their version of order. Fighting and killing, they thought, would fix everything and create the perfect new world order.

Not all fascists, like people, were created equal. Metaxas, the general of Greece, had dissolved parliament just as Mussolini and Hitler had, and was considered a fascist by definition. Rather than goals of territorial expansion, murder or war, his intentions in dissolving parliament had been to reduce red tape in order to get the government to work better. Metaxas wanted to bring Greece back to a social and political level of past years, when Greece had influence in the Balkans. However, no portion of Metaxas's vision contained violence, murder, ethnic purging or war. His views for his country's growth and success were very different than those of Italy or Germany. He only wanted to better his country within its borders.

As World War II started, Greece was a simple country that did not have much to offer the outside world, aside from a rich history and a strategic military location. Greece had not been in Hitler's equation. He was on the verge of taking Russia.

Mussolini found himself in a downward spiral of never-ending anger. Hitler was making progress quickly and easily. Mussolini did not have a military that came close to the Nazi's, and he found himself being left behind in Hitler's efforts. They had once been colleagues, and Mussolini thought that Italy and Germany together would one day rule all of Europe. Mussolini had to figure out a way to win somewhere and show Hitler his power so he could regain the respect and equality they once shared. His opportunity was slipping away as the Nazis swept across Europe.

Mussolini reached desperately for a military victory. A report stated that English ships and planes were being given safe harbor and supplies in Greece. Whether or not this news was truth or propaganda, no one was sure. But Mussolini wrote to Hitler offering the use of Italian land and air forces, if and when the time came to attack Great Britain. Hitler politely declined, sighting it too difficult to supply the two armies because Italy did not have enough planes, tanks and weapons to support them. Mussolini had gotten the final slap on the face from his old friend and decided he had taken his last insult. His grand plan was for Hitler to see this headline in the papers: "Mussolini Occupies Greece."

Mussolini thought since Greece was small, and its leader a fellow fascist, the country would succumb easily to his demands.

The attack date was set for October 28, 1940. Prime Minister Metaxas received an ultimatum in writing from Mussolini and had only a few hours to respond. He was told to surrender immediately and the Greek people would not suffer casualties.

Mussolini could not have been more wrong about Greece's willingness to surrender. Metaxas replied without giving it much thought, with one word only: *"OXI!"* (NO!) The Greek mantra, "freedom or death," was ignited once again, with the same strong spirit as when they fought to gain independence from the Ottomans in 1821. March twenty-fifth has always been a big celebration throughout Greece. It marks the last day of Turkish Muslim rule, Independence Day. It was the first day I saw fireworks in the sky. It is certainly a big celebration, not only for Greece but for the Christian world. During Muslim rule, practicing Christianity was forbidden. Religion went underground and was taught in caves nestled in the mountains, called *krifo scholios* (secret schools). Since Greece had to keep its official Orthodox religion intact through invading Turks, Arabs and Mongols, churches fought hard to preserve their faith. Orthodoxy was never permitted to change or evolve. Greece once again, would have guard their way of life against Mussolini's regime.

A human's will to survive is inherently strong, and the will to preserve a *way* of life can sometimes be even stronger. A *way* of life surpasses your time on earth, and continues to thrive for many generations. With this knowledge, we can justify fighting for something, even dying for it. I wonder if this is why Greece's conflicts never seem to end for long; they will not allow any country or culture to invade or change them.

On the ship, I decide to find my room and rest. It is tiny, but the only place I can be alone. I have a terrible headache. Thinking about my life, I realize that the first vivid memories I have are of Greece entering the war and the events that transpired through it. How did we survive? Of course I know the answer to that question. *My mother.*

War (1940), Seven Years Old

I remember it all like it happened yesterday. It was October, a beautiful month. The air was cool, crisp and clean. I was seven. I played with my favorite doll alongside my mother as she cooked dinner. As I swaddled her in a blanket, I sang and rocked her by the fire.

"My *Tzitzika* Eleni, you have such a beautiful voice… keep on singing for me while I make dinner, please?" my mother asked as she kissed my forehead. At the sink, she chopped up vegetables to make a hearty soup. The *tzitzikas* had stopped singing in the trees.

Summer was over. I continued to sing where they left off for my mother.

Home was small, cozy, safe and secure. I sang to my baby as I created a makeshift crib out of two chairs pushed together.

"Do you want to listen to the radio, love?" my mother asked.

"Yes, please *Mama!*" I squealed in delight.

She turned the dial and tuned in to our favorite station. I put my baby doll down to sleep so that I could dance around the kitchen table. My mother smiled wide. She joined me and soon we spun in circles together. Laughter erupted between us. I twirled around her finger until I was dizzy. My mother's face floated above me and the floor felt slanted. I closed my eyes and laughed harder. My mother took a deep breath as she took in all of my childhood innocence and excitement. Taking photographs with her mind was something I often caught my mother doing when she looked at me. She preserved our moments in her own personal reservoir. I thought she was silly and funny and I loved it.

"*Mama* – are you taking pictures?" I asked. It was one of the jokes we shared. She knew how fleeting time was, how things would not be this way forever. After kissing my head, my mother broke away from the dance to get dinner ready. My father would be home from work any moment.

Suddenly the music stopped. The broadcaster announced: "Greece has been asked to surrender to Mussolini's army. Reports tell us that President Metaxas told him "No!" without a moment's hesitation. Ladies and Gentlemen: This means we are going to war with the Italians come midnight."

My mother's mouth dropped along with the bowl she was holding. It shattered across the floor. Porcelain shards were everywhere. But my mother did not move. She stood frozen for what felt like a long time. The first movement she made was the sign of the cross over her body and she started to pray. Then she put her head in her hands and sighed. I could not understand what happened. I was mad the radio stopped playing music and I had to stop dancing. I tentatively approached her, hands outstretched as my shoes further pulverized the porcelain into finer dust. She grabbed my hand and pulled me to her.

"It's alright, *koukla-mou* (my doll), *kardia-mou* (my heart)," she said as she stroked my hair. "We will be alright."

The radio announcer said we would be at war soon. I had never seen war and could not grasp what this meant for us, although I could sense from my mother that something terrible had just happened. Everything was about to change, and I was blissfully innocent and oblivious to it all.

My father came home, ranting and angry. My mother looked at me and silenced him.

"Not in front of Eleni, Kosta. Let's talk about this after she goes to bed," she said in a low voice. My parents shielded me as best they could, but every woman, man and child could not be protected from the truth.

After dinner, I fell into a deep but brief sleep. Soon I was awakened by voices. Friends and relatives had gathered in the streets. Some of the young men laughed in a celebratory way. It seemed almost as if they would be going to a fair and not a war. "Mussolini doesn't scare us! We're going to drive them out to the sea!" they chanted.

It was the middle of the night and people became energized. The men acted brave but their women cried. They realized their husbands and sons would have to fight and might even die.

Yesterday had been a normal day, with work, neighborhood gossip and mundane tasks. Suddenly, people were waiting for the moment Italian military troops would move in. How quickly life can change. It did not take the Italians long to cross into Greece from the Albanian mountains.

Sirens sounded in the streets so loud they made my ears hurt and the hair stand up on my arms. Their screeching sound surely woke up any soul that had managed to sleep through the commotion in the streets.

An army truck drove slowly throughout my neighborhood. A young man with a megaphone made an announcement: "All men under forty years and able, come out of your homes and join us. We are at war and we need your help. Come protect your country." Men took to the streets and marched alongside the man with the megaphone, some were still wearing their pajama pants and nightcaps.

They chanted Metaxas's answer to Greece's surrender: "*Oxi! Oxi! Oxi!*"

I woke up the next morning to my parents making a fuss around the house. My father had just come back from shopping. My mother was busy making a pot of coffee. I stepped into the kitchen sleepy-eyed. My father glided over to my mother who had just sat down at the table.

"*Kardia-mou*, there is no easy way to say this – but I think you already know what I am about to tell you, don't you?" he asked.

"I bought plenty of groceries for you both. I think I bought all of the rice in the store. This should get you and Eleni through for a while."

My mother nervously poured her coffee and stirred the sugar without looking up.

"Vasiliki, please."

He put his finger under her chin and tilted her face up. When he looked at her eyes, they were full of tears. Before he had told her, my mother already knew. My father had gone and enlisted himself to fight. She did not argue with him or try to change his mind. She understood that there was nothing to discuss.

"When do you leave?" she asked.

"Now," my father told her.

My mother frantically gathered some things for his trip, her hands shaking. She handed him bread, cheese and olives wrapped in a white towel.

"Come back to me, Kosta," she demanded.

"*Agapi-mou* (my love), you know I will try my best. If God is willing then I will come back to you both," he replied.

"Don't say it like that, Kosta. You *will* come back. I *know* you will."

As she touched his cheek, I noticed my parents had tears in their eyes. I was used to seeing them together, happy and never sad like this. The sight of their pain tore at my child-sized heart.

My father bent down to where I was standing, his only child. I stared painfully up at his face. He took me by the shoulders and kissed me on both cheeks over and over then hugged me, lifting me up.

"Take care of your *Mama* for me, please," he whispered in my ear.

"Of course, *Papa*," I replied, not entirely sure what how I was supposed to take care of my mother.

Mama always takes care of *me*. But I realized it was not a time for questions. I was sure I would figure it all out later. Then he left us... with the clothes on his back, a photograph of me and my mother and the determination to fight for our Greece.

My parents embraced once more before he started down the street. He tried his best not to look back and walked straight and tall as if he was already a soldier. Hardening his heart and not allowing any sensitivity to weaken him was essential to his survival. He turned the corner at the end of our street, without looking back, and then he was gone.

A Cicada's Childhood

As a young cicada enters childhood, she is still too young to use her wings, but she is anxious to begin something new, to fly free in the world. She starts notice the world around her, in all its ugliness, and in all its beauty.

Days After

The days that followed *Papa's* leaving were hard. Many other families were in the same position, yet it did not make my mother and I feel any better. The women learned quickly to lean on one another for both emotional and physical support. My daily activities remained the same. I still ran around with my cousins until dark. I still went to school every day. Though a war had begun, most children did not notice any difference other than the fact one or more men were missing from their lives, and that sometimes their mother's cried.

One morning, as I walked with my cousins Eleni, Thanasi, Yiorgos, Adonis and Thanasi's friend, Yianni, Adonis looked at me and smiled. I knew what he was thinking.

"Adonis, come on. Today? Isn't it a little *dangerous* with the war going on? What if we are not in school and something important happens? How will we know?" I asked.

"Oh don't be so afraid of everything, *Tzitzika*," he replied.

If there was ever a perfect day to skip class and enjoy the warm fall sunshine, it was today. We all decided that if we made sure we got home at the usual time our mothers expected us, there should be no problems. We headed to the park. My heart sank when we reached it. The kid we dreaded in school was there. We called him the *Diavolos* (the devil). There could not have been a name more appropriate. He was sitting on a swing with two of his friends, smoking cigarettes. For some reason, he disliked me a lot. I gulped. I hated *Diavolos* and I hated cigarettes. I loved animals and he thought it was fun to torture them. I have heard the stories but never seen him do it. He entertained himself with the suffering of innocent stray cats and dogs. Bile rose in my mouth. It is almost as if he immediately sensed my weakness, my innocence, my love of animals. Before I could look away, his eyes locked onto mine.

"*Tzitzika*. Little bug. You know what? I hate animals...but I *especially* hate insects. I squash them all of the time!" he said. I gulped and my palms grew sweaty.

Diavolos was bigger than most of us. He was the same age as Adonis, in the same class. Still, *Diavolos* had a good foot over Adonis. Adonis stepped towards *Diavolos* about to speak when Yianni stepped in front of me, offering his protection. I couldn't hold back the burning tears that started to form. I was embarrassed.

"Yianni, is she your girlfriend now?" *Diavolos* asked, laughing with a snort. His two friends chuckled along. Adonis turned and gave Yianni a look that clearly asked: *What are you doing?*

Fists flew between the six boys: *Diavolos* and his two friends against Yianni, Adonis and Thanasi. *Diavolos* punched Yianni's mouth and then Yianni punched him in the nose hard. Streams of blood ran down both his nostrils. He wiped it with the sleeve of his shirt and looked at me as he said: "Come on, she is not worth it." My heart was racing. I ran over to Yianni where he was holding his hand over his mouth.

"Are you alright?" I asked.

"Don't worry, *Tzitzika*. Those boys are just a bunch of fools. Don't ever listen to a thing they say."

As he pulled his hand away, I noticed his lip was purple and swollen.

"Oh, no, your lip is already getting big. You need to put something cool on it," I said.

"How, Eleni? Go home? Our parents will kill us. It will be alright. I'll tell my mother I hit it on the playground at school."

He looked at me and smiled with a flinch. He must have been in a lot of pain. Worry flashed from my eyes to his.

"Don't worry, Eleni *Tzitzika*. I told you, I am fine. After all, protecting you is worth it."

My cheeks burned.

Adonis came up from behind him and punched him in the back.

"Stay away from my cousin, Yianni. She is just a little girl," he said.

"You are the only little girl I see here, Adonis," Yianni responded. They started to pretend fight with each other. I laughed because I loved being with all of them. My cousin Eleni sat under the shade of a large olive tree and I joined her.

"Let's stay here and we can eat our lunch under this tree. *Diavolos* and his friends won't come back, we'll have this place to ourselves all day." Eleni said.

We feasted on the bread and cheese our mother's had packed for us. Quickly the episode faded and laughter replaced all fear. All was forgotten.

After lunch, I hopped onto the merry-go-round with Eleni while Adonis and Thanasi pushed. We spun faster and faster and we laughed so hard. I caught a glimpse of Yianni sitting pensively at the bottom of the slide, looking at a flower in his hand. I stared, wanting to know what he was thinking. Suddenly, my hands were not holding on the bars and my body was flying high through the air. I landed with a thud, directly beneath the merry-go-round. It swirled above me close and fast. I was pinned. I heard the boys yelling and Eleni screaming. It was only seconds but it felt like it took hours to for it to stop. I rolled out and Eleni helped me to my feet. She brushed dirt off my clothes. I was so shocked by the event, I did not even have time to cry. I could not find the emotion or words to express my fear.

"*Tzitzika*, why the hell did you let go?" Adonis scolded. "What were you thinking?"

"I don't know," I admitted. I really didn't know what happened to me. One minute I was looking at Yianni with the flower. I saw his fat purple lip then I heard his words in my head: "You are worth it." Those words made my heart flutter and I felt dizzy. The next moment I was flying through the air. How could I even begin to explain that to my cousins?

"I'm fine. I don't know how, but my hands slipped. But I am not hurt," I told them.

I looked up and my eyes met Yianni's for a moment. I cringed when I saw that his lip looked even worse. But on the inside I was smiling as my mind repeated his sweet declaration: "Protecting you is *worth it*."

Italy (1940)

Greece's population was approximately seven times smaller than Italy's. The Italian's number of soldiers and quantity of firepower was ten times more than what Greece had. But there was something left uncalculated that the Italian fascist army could not buy or supply themselves with; the character of the Greek people. The Greeks defended their homeland fearlessly.

A popular vocalist named Sofia Vembou had written lyrics about the war, poking fun at the Italians: "With a smile on their lips our boys go to war, and the Italians run as they give them what they asked for!" Greece made it clear that they would not be defeated. They would fight to the end just as they had in every battle before. Character is stronger than weapons when used correctly.

Spirituality

Spiritual strength is important. The dangerous realities of war made Greek soldiers nervous, but they also had the knowledge in their hearts that as Christians, this life is not the permanent one. They believed in eternal life in the kingdom of heaven. This is what gave the soldiers strength and the ability to put their lives on the line. They fought for every generation past, present and future; for all of the people who have lived on this land, who currently do and who will one day. Above all, the Greeks were prideful. If they were going to die, they would do so on their terms, not by surrendering to any foreign occupation.

Papa's Absence

While my father was off fighting, my mother assumed all responsibilities. She found many different ways to fix our home and fill our table with food. She worked odd jobs whenever she could. Before the war, my father had opened a small *kafineon* (coffee shop), with my *Theo* Panayotis in Omonia Square in the center of Athens. *Mourias*, named for the region of Greece my father's side of the family lived before they moved to Athens a few generations back. I helped my parents occasionally. I hated walking through the fog of smoke. Almost every man had a cigarette in one hand, black coffee in the other. My father smoked as well. My mother hated it, constantly complaining about the smell. My father brought in different bands who plucked the most nostalgic, heart wrenching music on their bouzouki strings. I sang and danced. My father and his friends would get down on one knee and clap for me.

It had always been my father's dream to own that *kafineon*. Men would come to twirl worry beads in their hands and talk of politics, religion, life and death. To my father's dismay, his dream had come to fruition at the wrong time. When the war began, he knew people would have no extra money for entertainment and my father had no idea how long it would last. My father for forfeited his dream job to fight. Giving it up was not a choice, it was necessary. Before he left, the doors to *Mourias* were closed immediately and indefinitely.

It did not take long, after the war began, for the good news to spread: the Italians were being driven back to the border of Greece and into Albania. We knew that is where my father was stationed. My mother was proud, and a small glimmer of light and hope started to show in her eyes.

Young Italian soldiers seemed to remind Greek mother's of their own sons. The Italians that the Greeks captured and held as prisoners of war could hardly be called "prisoners." They began to dance, eat and drink together with the Greek people. Most of the Italians did not want to fight, and were happy to be pulled out of battle to spend their time as prisoners.

Imagine – people feeling sorry and showing hospitality for the army that was invading them? This had to be unprecedented. It did not seem right that one dictator's decisions led to war, but this was politics and the power that came along with it. These young men had no choice, they were to do as their country demanded of them.

Thalia, a girl from our neighborhood, met an Italian solider named Alessio. He spotted her on his rounds. They fell in love, despite the fact they lacked a common language.

"It is so much better that way, if you ask my opinion!" *Thea* Maritsa said as she giggled with my mother. "They don't even have the means to fight. I have often thought about how nice it would be if my husband had nothing to say sometimes. How nice that would be indeed!" They both laughed so hard, they had to hold on to one another by the shoulders to stand. Their laughter and friendship always made me feel warm and happy inside.

Last Attempt

The Italians made one last effort to overpower the Greeks. On April 6, 1941, Italy conducted a six day attack using every weapon, plane and tank possible. But alas, Greek passion overpowered the Italian number of soldiers and equipment. Mussolini had to ask Hitler for help. Hitler was infuriated that Italy retreated into Albania and saw them as traitors for giving up so easily. Sending troops to Greece drained Hitler's resources for taking Russia, the next country on his agenda. Hitler's carefully laid plans were destroyed before his eyes and it was all Mussolini's fault.

Hitler went after the Italians aggressively. Some Greek people took pity on them and helped hide them in their homes. The Greeks saw how similar they were in culture; how much they valued God, family and good food. Many friendships formed out of supposed enemies as the Greeks helped save them from the enemy that they now both feared together.

Germany (1941-1945)

These are the details I recall from the start of the German invasion: One night, a loud noise shook our neighborhood. I was in bed but had not fallen asleep yet. Suddenly, a force nearly knocked me to the ground. *Earthquake!* I thought to myself, as I stumbled out of bed and ran to find my mother. Our bodies collided in the hallway with a loud *thud*. I found relief in her arms. My theory of being caught in an earthquake quickly disintegrated when I realized there were no aftershocks, only an eerie silence. It was an explosion.

Loud, impatient knocks were soon at our door. Startled, my mother gasped as we walked together. I could not believe how the door had splintered and cracked from the blast. The shutters on our windows had been blown open and were flapping in the night breeze. My *Theo* Stathis's voice called to us nervously.

"Open up, it's me, Stathis," he said.

My *Theo*, my favorite. He loved me so much, he sometimes called me his "eye," a high compliment of adoration. Your eyes are one of the most important things you possess, at least physically. I bet that is why it was a common term of endearment. There was even this song called, "I love you more than my eyes," that he sang to me. He never had a daughter of his own.

When my mother opened the door, my poor *theo* looked like a startled animal in fight-or-flight mode. I had never seen him like this before. His dark brown, tanned skin was the color of chalk. He scanned both of us with short, panicked breaths. Seeing we were both fine, he took a deep breath.

"They have bombed Piraeus, Vasiliki. The port is destroyed. It is not the Italians, though. This is the work of Hitler. The Germans are here now. We are at war... with... the Nazi's!"

My mother let out a shriek before covering her mouth with one hand tightly. Her eyes were wide as she tried to muffle the uncontrollable screams that erupted out of her.

Like an angry volcano without warning, ready to swallow the island of Santorini, my mother's mind became   clouded with fire, ash and fear. I realized she did not want to frighten me, and held her best possible composure. But I was frightened, very frightened.

Piraeus was only a few miles from where we lived. It was the main sea port. All transportation of people to the islands, and goods to and from the country, landed there.

"Now that we are cut off from our connection to everywhere else... I don't know what will happen. Our worst fears for the direction of this war are upon us... We cannot stay here. You know we have to go to the mountains. *Right away!*" he told my mother.

Desperation filled her eyes as she stared at him in disbelief. I knew she was panicking about my father, what would happen to him now? I wondered. As my *theo* was excitedly talking, pacing and strategizing, I could not help but focus on the far-away look in my mother's eyes. All she could think of was my *papa*.

Sirens blared in the streets. People closed their shutters and blinds with violent snaps. Chaos and panic erupted. Hitler would be marching in with his troops in no time. Would it be days? Weeks? Hours? Minutes? There was no way to predict it.

The women cried and crossed themselves over and over, mumbling prayers, exclaiming *"Kyrie Elison* (Lord have mercy)!"

The Greeks were prepared to keep on fighting. However, there was no laughing or joking about the Germans. This was different. Every last person was already mourning the loss of life they knew would come. The sky was dark. Even the clouds were black and ready to cry. The sky over Greece turned grey with us. The men went to sign up for the military slowly, like they were in a funeral procession. Outside the door to our homes there sat a coiled snake. Venomous. Waiting and ready to strike. You can never tell by looking at the ugly creature when it will attack, but if you get too close it is inevitable. The Nazi attack was near. We were waiting, they were waiting. The snake would strike. The pain of the bite would settle in, and poison our blood. Chance of survival was unknown.

With sirens blaring outside, my mother took me in her lap and wrote to my father before it was too late. She had to send a letter immediately in hopes she would hear back from him one last time. Once this new wave of war began, she did not know when or if she would hear from her husband again. She swallowed hard, and let me sit in her lap as she wrote.

Dear Kosta,

My love. The bombs have shaken our home badly tonight. The front door nearly split in two. I am not sure whether or not we should wait it out here or head to the horyo. How bad are things there? I am so afraid... Are the Germans already there? Tell me what I should do. I will wait for your direction. I love you always. Please, please be careful.

Love,

Vasiliki

She sealed the envelope with a kiss and wiped a single tear from her eye. *Theo* Stathis had gone downstairs for a few moments then came back even more frenzied.

"Start packing. We leave at dawn tomorrow," he said.

"Stathis, you know I cannot leave. Not until I hear back from Kosta," my mother insisted.

"Vasiliki, you are not being reasonable! We have to take the kids somewhere safe," he said in an aggravated tone.

"My house is safe. I need to make sure Kosta knows where we are. Please, Stathis."

"Listen, I understand you need to hear from him, but if he comes back here before you do, he will know where to look for you," he argued.

"What if he doesn't? What if he thinks something has happened to us? I can't do this! Don't ask me again, please. I have made my decision. I will not leave here until Kosta tells me to," she said.

Nervous beads of sweat formed on my uncles forehead.

"Let me take Eleni for you, then," he offered.

"No. We stay together," my mother insisted. She crossed her arms and shook her head back and forth.

"You are more stubborn than a donkey!" he told her, shaking his head.

"I can't..." my mother said.

"Your sister will be upset. Think about her, too," he begged.

"My answer is... No. Please don't be mad," my mother asked.

"You! You *women*! You are all the same. Crazy. You all make me crazy!" he yelled as he slammed the door behind him.

My family on both sides left for the *horyo* the next morning. Even the tears of my mother's baby sister did not move her to change her mind. My mother would not bend. She refused to leave her husband behind.

Kosta's Perspective (1941)

The air is silent. How long has it been? In these mountains, in the wilderness, close to the border of Albania, I have lost all concept of time. It has been at least two days since we set up camp. Day and night mesh together as one. I am on constant alert, so I never sleep. The nights are getting cold, and I am always hungry. The mornings are hardest with bones and joints so chilled I am stiff.

The men and I sat to rest, our backs against the jagged stone when a loud noise rips rough the clouds above. Planes fly overhead. They shake the ground where we sit. They are too high to shoot and we are afraid to move. We do not want to become targets. Frozen in silence, they pass overhead, opening fire on the ground below. We lean into the rock and take cover. Everyone is shouting as chaos erupts. I close my eyes and see only her, Vasiliki. Some men fall, dead and bleeding on the ground. I think, this could be the end for me, for all of us in a few short moments. My God, now the Italians have planes... I did not think they had these in their artillery. In a horrifying moment, the planes descend lower, revealing swastikas painted in red and white. Panagia, mother of God. Have mercy on us! The Germans! As quickly as they appeared, they depart. I stare at the scene of death which surrounds me and think: this is beginning of the end. I have to write to my sweet Vasiliki before it is too late.

Leaving Athens

A few uneventful weeks went by in the city. My mother buzzed about, attending to her normal routine. Then, it was announced that school was closed indefinitely and the few kids who were left in my neighborhood were not allowed to run around outside and play. Everyone's shutters remained closed and tensions were high. My mother held on to her usual routine as a way to fool herself from the truth: we had to leave.

Finally, his letter arrived. When the postman came, I ran and snatched it from his hand, smiling and yelling for my mother.

"*Mama! Mama!* It's the letter from *Papa!* He has written to us!"

I scurried upstairs faster than a frightened cat and begged her to read it out loud.

"Dear Vasiliki,

My love. Please take Eleni and head to the horyo immediately. Do not hesitate. Things are not good here. The Italians were not successful and now the Germans are moving in (though you probably know already as you read this). I do not think we will be able to hold them back…. they are just too strong for us. Yesterday they sent planes to drop bullets and bombs on top of us. Before they fired, I thought… they were magnificent. Tell Eleni that I saw planes that buzzed and flew like tzitzikas and that they made me think of her. I am always thinking of her. This is the only war story I have to share, and I am sorry that it is not a good one. The men who are with me are strong in mind and body, and we are doing our best. How I wish I could fly and take you and Eleni far away from here. I am afraid the worst is yet to come… So go. I will know where to find you. I love you. Please always know that. I will be home to you both soon. But if something should happen - don't let Eleni forget her father and how much he loved her, please my sweet wife.

Love,

Kosta"

My mother immediately grabbed every suitcase and tattered bag we had so she could pack as much of our home as possible. She was sobbing and packing at a frantic pace. She worked hard into the night preparing our things and any food we had. The next morning we were headed for the train station. My mother was relieved that they had communicated this one last time and he would not come back from war frenzied at our disappearance.

We exited our beautiful home with its marble steps, beautiful flowers and patches of *vasiliko* thriving. My mother closed the door, did the sign of the cross and took one long, deep breath. She almost made it down the stairs when she asked me to wait for a moment and she ran back inside. She returned, with her wedding photo was clutched under her arm.

"Let's go," she said, taking my hand.

Train

We started our dangerous six hour train ride up the mountains as the Germans moved across the border into Greece simultaneously. The train was old, dirty, bumpy, hot and reeked of body odor. Fear was so strong, most people seemed to be unaware of the conditions that surrounded them. This was not the time to be complaining. Keeping our families safe was each and every person's one and only concern. Nothing else mattered.

It was not too long into the ride when we all heard the most horrific sounds. Loud planes flew low to the ground. I covered my ears. The planes were nothing compared to the sound of the bombs when they landed, which shook us like an earthquake.

"Oh God. It's the Germans!" people shouted. Everyone cried and crossed themselves. My mother stiffened.

We heard the screeching of the planes and the explosion of bombs once again. *No! No! No!* I screamed inside my head, too scared to make a sound. I looked up at my mother, not wanting to believe that our situation was real. *Why would these people try to hurt us? Had we done something wrong?*

The shrieking sound the bombs made before they hit the earth were ghastly. My hair stood straight up on my arms as body tensed, waiting for another explosion. My mother remained composed, standing strong as I stood enveloped in her muscular arms; arms born from years of working hard in the fields and in our home. Beautiful arms. Wouldn't it be miraculous, I thought to myself, if an earthquake occurred during all of this, opening up a vast crack in the earth where we would be swallowed and saved from danger? Beneath our feet the rickety train rattled on.

My body shook involuntarily. Every time the planes screamed over us, I was unprepared for the sound. They screeched like nails down a chalkboard, amplified by a thousand times. A disturbing image came into my mind. A mischievous person holding a balloon in one hand and a pin in another. The anticipation was almost unbearable. The balloon was going to pop, but when? I imagined this awful person doing that over and over; someone with a never ending supply of balloons. No matter how hard I tried, I could not see this imaginary person's face. A dark cloud hung over it, not allowing me to see.

The bombs reminded me of fireworks, which I had seen on a few happy occasions in my life. I closed my eyes, trying to remember how magical the glowing embers looked as they floated down from the sky. I remembered how my mouth hurt from smiling so wide for so long.

I also tried to remember other happy things, like dancing. I was never happier than when I found myself weaving in and out of the circle formed by everyone holding hands. I would spin my white handkerchief in the air, laughing. I saw my father's face, full of pride, clapping and whistling on one knee as I twirled and sang for him.

Thick, black smoke poured into the windows. My sudden coughing fit snapped me out of remembering. The windows had to be opened every few minutes to listen for planes. We listened in silence, and if we heard anything, the conductor would slam on the brakes and we were to evacuate immediately.

Another loud explosion ripped through the air. I wondered: *Where did it hit? What about my papa? Could he be hurt, killed?*

My mother held me in a tight embrace; her stance steady and strong. Her unwavering composure gave nothing away, as usual. I knew that she was being strong for me. She had on her "strong face" to show me everything was not as horrid and unpredictable as it seemed.

I looked around the train. Many of the cheeks were tear-streaked. I observed one woman, struggling not make a sound so hard she was choking herself. She had three young children hanging on her. She remained stoic, but her eyes were like stormy oceans, churning relentlessly with fear. Mothers, tired and scared, did not want their children to be afraid. They turned their eyes away, praying they would not see the truth in them. Perhaps they thought if they acted calm, strong and sure, their children would sense nothing. Yet all is clear to a child, like the distinctive smell that wafted through the air – the smell of nervous sweat. How quickly adults forget how intuitive children are; how they once were themselves.

Another explosion rattled the tracks and shook the train as planes screamed overhead. "Evacuate!" That was the last word I heard before chaos erupted. There was darkness and panic as people pushed each other out of the train doors. My mother and I ran into the olive groves, hand-in-hand clutching a small sack of food.

"But *Mama* – I want my doll!" I screamed. I had left her on my seat in the confusion. It was my one and only play thing that I had with me. I worried I might have lost her forever. Tears pooled in my eyes. My mother had no time to soothe me. With a tight grip she held my wrist and yanked hard.

"There is no time! Run, *agapi-mou*. RUN!" She screamed. We ran, until we were hidden by a significant amount of trees and brush and waited. I cried so hard for my poor baby doll, it made my head ache. My mother and I sat on the ground and I rested my head against her chest. I was not sure how much time had passed. I thought I had closed my eyes for only a moment, but suddenly we were making our way back to the train, my mother carrying me in her arms. As we approached the train, a young girl was attracting everyone's attention. She was making a speech and everyone came closer to hear it.

"I have an idea that might help us: get as many branches as you can from these trees. Lay them on the top of the train. Does anyone have rope?" Everyone gathered branches, belts, yarn, scarves, whatever they had and covered the roof. It was a genius idea. We ran to the train with branches held high in our hands, smiling. Like the little dove after the great flood, we held our olive branches. It was our way of saying: *Look, you wondered whether or not I would find land and safety, but here I am. I am alive. There is hope yet. Even the great flood ended.*

We all made our way back on the train where I found my baby doll, waiting. I looked at my mother with big eyes and a wide smile. I giggled as I grabbed and hugged her tight, a moment of light in our dark world. My mother stared at me, smiling.

Soon, the train was moving again. We ran many times back into the olive groves and wheat fields. I made sure I held my doll in my arms every moment. It was ironic how my old playground would save our lives, that the branches of the trees I ran through with my cousins in laughter were used to save us from something sinister.

The train moved slowly. The air was full of noise as planes flew over us from all directions. Over and over this dramatic run for our lives continued. I felt like it would never end.

Back on the train, I sat with my head on my mother's lap. My thoughts drifted and my eyes closed as the skies grew quiet. Exhaustion consumed every one of us, and I succumbed to sleep until our last stop.

Horyo

Theo Stathis was waiting for us at the station with two horses. "*Matia-mou!* (my eye!)" he said, hugging me tightly.

"Stathis…" my mother said, hugging him tight. She wiped tears from her tired eyes.

He shook his head in sympathy and probably frustration that my mother had waited so long to leave the city. He could tell we had a bad trip. He put me and my mother on one of the horses and strapped our luggage to the other. Grabbing both of the horses, he walked us to our home in the *horyo*. My *theo* had horses because no one dared to attract attention with the lights and noise of vehicles. I crinkled my nose. The horses stank! I imagined my mother, her siblings, and her parents riding donkeys all the way down and back up the mountains to get to the city, down skinny dirt roads, as rocks crumbled off the edge. Although I had always rolled my eyes when my mother told me how hard things were when she was a child in a world without trains, this trip I would have strongly preferred the donkey.

Soon we reached our family's home in Klitora. This is the home my mother grew up in, where her own mother died giving birth. It is the home she left as a young bride to become a city girl. My mother took a nostalgic deep breath and a long exhale when she opened the front door. Stepping inside, everything was as we left it; frozen in time, a better time for our family last summer before war began. We stood before the same broken, but functional, staircase, old furniture and musty smell of closure. The simple house contained a few necessary rooms.

"I am glad you made it out safely," my *theo* said as he carried a few bags inside for us. "You cut it close, Vasiliki," he said, as he shook his head at her.

"I know, but everything is fine and now Kosta knows exactly where to find us. I got a letter from him, telling us to come here. Thank you for picking us up," she said.

I wandered around the house, touching old familiar things. I stopped at the fireplace where my great-uncle left his initials on the mantle. He carved it before he went to war in 1820 against the Turks. "M.Y." Michalis Yiorgacopoulos. I traced his initials with my fingers. He was only sixteen my mother told me, and he signed up to fight. He felt so passionate, that he lied about his age. When he came home to tell his family, his father (my great-grandfather) fainted. He had a vision of him dead, in a dream, before he left. He knew he would never see his son again and he was right. He died in battle after a short time. There is so much history here, if only these walls, this mantle, these pictures and floors could speak. It would be so interesting to see the events that took place, see my grandparents and great-grandparents' faces and hear their voices. I have created them in my mind from the small bits of information I posses. Now there is a new war. I wondered: *What would they think of this one?*

I felt arms behind me. Of course they were my cousins. Hugging me from behind, picking me up were Yiorgos and Adonis. After hugs came the punches and the usual taunting boys find fun. I laughed. In came my *Thea* Maritsa holding baby Vangeli in her arms, scolding Yiorgos and Adonis. She hugged and kissed us frantically, thankful that we made it out of the city alive. My little happy, roly-poly one-and-a-half year old cousin Vangeli was messy with drool dripping from his mouth. I loved to care for him and help my *thea*.

"Oh, Vangeli, what has become of you just a short time without me?" I asked him. I kissed his chubby cheeks and he giggled. I grabbed a napkin and wiped his mouth.

"Thank you, Eleni. I know I can always count on my sweet niece to keep Vangeli in order," *Thea* Maritsa said. "Come, next door to eat before you unpack. I made string beans with feta cheese and tomato sauce," she told us. My mouth watered as we walked into their house and sat at the table.

My *Thea* Maria and *Theo* Panayotis were a few villages over, in Meseca with my cousins Eleni and Thanasi. I miss them and wonder when we will get to see them. I have no idea where my friend Yianni has gone, but he and his family left before my mother and I, and I am sure he is somewhere in these mountains. Thanasi would probably know. I closed my eyes and imagined Yianni safe, wherever he was. The only people left in the city were those who had no connections in the *horyo*. They were the most unfortunate because they were trapped in the middle of the Nazi occupation. They had marched into Athens hours after my mother and I had left. A curfew was instituted immediately. If you went outside after five o'clock in the evening, you would be shot dead.

After we ate, I looked at Adonis and laughed at the sight of his mischievous grin. I got up from my chair and chased him. We ran outside through the open fields, rolling in the grass, laughing like clucking chickens until it was dark.

I came home to find my mother still working on the house. She had worked hard all day to make our summer house feel like home in Athens. Sheets, curtains and tablecloths blew outside in the breeze by moonlight. The clothes had dried to a hard, crisp texture from being bleached in the sun all day. My mama kissed my forehead and asked: "*Koukla* (doll), will you please help me take this laundry in?"

"Of course, Mama," I smiled. My mother loaded a small pile of sheets and clothes into my arms. The moon reflected off my arm full of white cotton, glowing so bright, it felt as if I had plucked the moon from the sky and was holding it in my arms. I looked up. Stars twinkled above us, and I could hear crickets chirping in the tall grass. The night was so peaceful and soothing after the awful train ride we had to endure. In the *horyo*, I felt closer to God than anywhere else. I wondered if my *papa* was looking at the same stars and moon at the same moment. "*Mama* – when is *Papa* coming back? Is he coming to meet us here?"

"I don't know, sweetie. I wish I had the answer." She was worried about my papa and I knew my asking wasn't going to make it better. I had to know whether or not she knew something. After seeing the anguished look in her eyes, I promised myself I would never ask her again.

I felt safe in the *horyo*. At least I was allowed to run and play outside. My mother remained on guard for us, always worried, thinking through every possible next move, depending on the variety of situations that may or may not arise. My mother tried her best to gather any information on my father's whereabouts without success. There had been no communication between my mother and father since we had arrived in the *horyo*. It felt like he was gone forever.

One day, despair got the better of my mother's strength when the radio announcer said: "Ladies and Gentlemen of our great country. This is the last you will hear from me or any Greek radio station. In the morning, when you tune in, you will be hearing German. Be safe, be strong and God bless." That was the last radio broadcast we understood for a while.

Anxiety filled the space around us. The storm that had been lingering had finally hit us full force and nobody knew how much damage it would do before it was over. No one was safe. Life became more unpredictable and precious than ever. Luckily in the *horyo*, we were removed, out of the enemies view.

My mother never feared for herself, and as soon as we got settled, she wanted to help others. Since crops and animals were abundant in our *horyo*, my mother decided to make the dangerous trip back and forth to

Athens to share with family and friends who needed it desperately.

"I cannot just sit here, knowing our neighbors and friends are hungry in the city," she told my *thea*. "But you cannot save the world, Vasiliki. Why do you have to be such a risk-taker? Why can't you just hide here with us until it is over?" she begged.

"Because I can't, Maritsa. How can I live with myself knowing I have something that can save lives?"

"Well, don't take Eleni. I will keep her safe here. Please. Do not linger there for long. People become mad and dangerous when they are desperate, and the Nazi's have no mercy," my *thea* said.

"Don't worry, Maritsa. I will be careful," my mother assured her.

The next day my mother went to *Athina*, which had plummeted deeper into famine than she could have ever anticipated.

Vasiliki's Perspective

Famine. Starvation. People lying dead in the streets. Some picking through garbage, hoping to find some scraps of food. Dirty, moaning crying people. My skin crawls as I carry my small sack through the city to my neighborhood. I wish I could help them all, but I know I cannot. The air stinks of decay, death. So many more will be dead before I even make it back to the horyo. Dear God. What is happening to my country?

My Kosta. Why did he have to volunteer to go right away? The war is going to be long, I can feel it. The less time he spends outside this winter the better chance he will survive. The winter is coming, and the war is only beginning. I remember the night before he left, as the sirens rang in the streets. We held each other close in bed, saying nothing. There were no words for how we felt. All that we could do was hold each other tight. In the morning, our entire world began to disintegrate. He left, and my heart is broken.

Athens

Within two months, approximately three-hundred thousand people died in the city. My mother made multiple trips into the heart of the horror. Most families were not even reporting the dead so they could continue to use their ration cards for food, though most days there was no food to distribute. At nighttime, the Germans executed hundreds of men they suspected were part of resistance groups. Rather than intimidate the Greeks into submission, the resistance groups grew stronger.

Making deliveries of food to Athens was a courageous mission. Miraculously, my mother made the train ride back and forth numerous times. Eventually, she got brave enough to take me with her. Sometimes she left me with *Thea* Maritsa and *Theo* Stathis. Sometimes, the soldiers would throw her off the train, because they could. She continued to get back on in different places until she was able to stay in a spot where no one paid her any attention.

German offices were set up in homes in Athens. House by house, they ordered the families to leave allowing them to take only the clothes upon their backs. The street behind mine, where many doctors, lawyers and politicians resided was taken over completely. They had everything and suddenly they had nothing. Once they were evacuated, a large gate was put at the end of the street, locked and guarded. The Germans helped themselves to any valuables and food they wanted. Soon there was almost no food for the city people. The most ironic thing was that the crops in Greece that year were great. However, there was no way to transport them into a city without infrastructure and with roads too damaged and dangerous for travel.

My mother had gotten back from another three day trip she took alone. I ran to her. She hugged and kissed me at least one hundred times.

"*Yiasas* (hello) Maritsa, Stathis. Was Eleni a good girl?" my mom asked.

"Always," my *theo* said, kissing me on top of my head. Even if I had been a little fresh, he would never tell.

"I have good news, Maritsa. Our homes remain untouched. They are sitting there just as we left them."

"Thank God, Vasiliki! Thank you, my beautiful sister," she said hugging her tightly. "Do me a favor, though. Don't go again too soon. I am so frightened each time you leave, I can hardly stand it."

My *thea* was too fearful to travel, especially with little Vangeli whom she could not leave behind. She nursed him constantly. Sometimes I thought he had become attached to her breast.

I remember nursing from my mother because it was not long ago. I did not stop until I was over three. I would ask her: "*Mama,* come here, please bring me your milk!" She tried desperately to get me to stop. My *thea* made fun of her for not being able to control me. Finally, my mother put some bitter liquid on her nipples. I ran off, spitting and trying to rub the taste off my tongue with my hands. I was convinced my mother's milk had gone sour, was ruined forever. I never asked for it again. My mother told me when I was older how it was one of the hardest things she had ever done, to sever the first bond we shared.

"But I have to be honest…" my mother continued.

"I don't know if it will last forever… our homes staying intact and unoccupied. The street behind ours, the one the Germans took over, is very dangerous. Last night I slept at home, and they were wild and drunk. They shot their rifles into the air all night."

"Do you remember the German family that lived on that street behind ours with the two daughters, remember them? The Friedberg's? They host parties for the Nazi's, with the most extravagant food and drinks you can imagine. People are dying of hunger in the streets, and it doesn't even make the Germans flinch. Our neighbor is having parties for our enemy. I have never seen anything like it," my mother told her. "I saw young children hopping the fence behind us to look in their trash. They sucked on the fish bones that the Germans had thrown out for cats to eat!"

Our German neighbors, who had been in Greece for years, were our friends. They got to remain in their home behind the new gated community because they were German and they had claimed loyalty to Hitler. Mr. Friedberg claimed the need to protect himself and his family when he saw his neighbors, he tried to explain, but nobody would speak a word to him again.

"The neighborhood will not allow him to stay in Greece after this. He will never step foot in Athens again once the war ends," my mother said.

"They betrayed us," Maritsa said.

"Maritsa, if the situation was reversed, wouldn't we do whatever we needed to in order to protect our families?" my mother asked.

"Who knows what would have become of them if they did not take the side of their own country? The Germans might have done something terrible to them too," my mother added. "Although, I would rather stand up for what I believed in than live a lie. If we are not true to ourselves, who are we, anyhow?" my mother said. She was right, and wise as usual about such things.

"My big sister. Always the brave one. I don't know if I would be able to fight like you. You have a special fire. That is why I admire you so much. You are so strong," Maritsa said as she took my mother's hands in hers and squeezed them. My mother was like my own personal saint; generous, full of love and deeply religious. She had great compassion and faith. She would have rather been burned or thrown to the lions than denounce truth.

There were not too many like her, daring to do what she did for others. I always swore when God made mothers he did something different and completely brilliant with mine. She always did what she believed was right; there was no falseness in her words or deeds.

"You never tell someone that you prayed really hard for them or for something or someone else," she once told me. At first I was puzzled. Would God really be upset if we shared what we had prayed for? My mother told me that we were not supposed to brag. The most faithful people keep these things between them and God. My mother told me that in charity, if you give to it in complete faith and compassion, you don't need to tell anyone about it. Did it matter if you did something for someone and they stole it, wasted it, or gave it away? Not at all, because the spirit in which you help another, that is what God judges, and you and God are the only ones who need to know you have done something good. That is why she was so private about what she prays for and what she does for others. I wanted to be just like her when I grew up.

As the situation in Athens became progressively worse, my mother was less likely to take me with her. One day, I had a crying fit about not being able to go. I heard people talking about the city getting worse and more dangerous than ever. I was afraid I might lose her and my *papa* both.

"Do you want me to be an orphan, *Mama*?" I screamed. She looked at me her blue eyes red and full of tears.

"Fine. Come with me. But listen. You *hold* my hand, *don't* speak to anyone. There will be *no* playing on the street. Most of your friends are gone. Home is very different now. Dangerous. Do you understand?" I looked at her with a smile and nodded my head. I didn't care about the danger waiting for us, I was happy she decided to take me.

We made our way to the packed train with our little bags of hard-boiled eggs, cheese and meat. My mother mumbled something about being lucky we were not mugged for our food. She told me that we were going to give it to the ones that were the hungriest first.

When we arrived, we walked down the streets littered with debris. My mother held my hand tight, catching every near fall as I stumbled over rubble. She was quick to steer me in the opposite direction of bodies both on the ground and hanging by ropes around their necks. Death was everywhere. I heard the ear-piercing cries of the women, all in black and on their knees, mourning their men. Their purple skinned bodies swayed from nooses eerily in the breeze. They prayed and they all asked the same question over and over: *why?* I finally understood why my mother had been coming to the city without me. I covered my ears to block out the sounds of sadness. It was enough to give anybody nightmares for the rest their life. War in all its horror was our reality.

As my mother and I walked among the streets of collapsed buildings, we walked in silence. How should a mother explain a war and violence with no reason? How could a mother explain to her only child that the world we lived in was one big, horrible mess? Finally she uttered the only explanation she could think of:

"I am sorry my love, this is war."

We reached our house with a sigh of relief. Everything looked untouched. My mother insisted we walk around the entire house to make sure it was safe. As nightfall approached, we fell asleep together on my parent's bed as she held me tight. Outside, bullets danced along with the stars and full moon. Each shot that rang out was probably an execution. We had become desensitized to certain things, I realized, because somehow, we managed to sleep.

Early the next morning, as the public trash collection trucks collected bodies my mother and I walked hurriedly to the train station. We had handed out every morsel of food aside from two hard-boiled eggs which my mother nestled safely in her pocket. She held on to my hand so tight, numbness began to take over. I did not say anything, I knew these trips made her nervous and this had been the worst trip by far. I was nervous, too.

Voula

As we made our way down the street, we noticed an old neighbor of ours, Voula. We had not known her very well but we recognized her as she came out of her front door. In shock, we realized her body had withered to skeletal proportions. Skin swimming over sharp bones was all that was left. She looked at us with a blank stare as she walked crookedly down her front steps. We thought she was calling to her children but she was talking to herself. She was alone.

"My husband – he went to sleep and my little ones… all my little ones, too… I could not save them. Where are they? Who has taken my family? Who has taken them? I need to find them… but I can't. Will no one help me? Will no one help me?" She walked up to my mother feebly grabbing her by the shoulders and said to her old neighbor. "My children, my husband… they have fallen asleep. They won't wake up. And now someone has taken them. Somehow. Somewhere. Can you help? Please help me!" she screamed weakly.

My mother grabbed hold of her and reached for the egg in her pocket which she frantically started to peel. Voula looked at my mother and weakly smiled.

"Vasiliki?" she asked, looking at my mother. Suddenly, Voula's eyes rolled before her body violently collapsed to the ground.

People came toward us and tried to help. A familiar thin man slapped Voula on the face, trying to wake her.

"If you go to sleep now, Voula… you will never wake up again. Don't let yourself sleep!

Tomorrow the bread will be distributed again. The officials promised. Just wait!" he pleaded.

The young man looked at my mother and shook his head. "Her whole family has died of starvation and she has gone completely mad. The entire city has picked clean all of the surrounding edible wild greens. You cannot even find a leaf to eat anymore. She will not survive much longer. Her heart will not bear it. What she really wants... is to be with her family."

My mother wrapped her hand around her wrist then put her ear to her mouth then chest. "She is gone," my mother whispered to the young man. He reached into the pocket of her dress for her food ration card. This may help him survive for a few more days if there would be bread to distribute.

"I am sorry, but if she is dead she does not need this," he said, tucking it into his pocket.

"Of course. I understand," my mother said.

"She is going to be picked up when the collector does his rounds. Leave her here. Trust me. There is nothing you can do."

The young man tipped his hat before he ran off. Wherever he went in this city, it could not have been anywhere good. There was no escape from the violence, hunger or madness in Athens.

But there was something my mother did that made Voula's death more civilized. She lifted the tiny woman's body and laid her on a bench, gently placing her hands over her chest. She looked like she was sleeping. Wherever she was, she was peaceful. I hoped that the climb to heaven was quick, and that she was already with her husband and children. Voula reminded me of my grandfather. My mother told me how he could hardly wait to meet her mother again in heaven. I understood in that moment, the wanting to die, the loneliness of being the last of your family left on earth. Voula was free.

That day in Athens, I came to understand war. Before I saw the bodies in the streets and Voula die before my eyes, I knew I did not like the Italians or the Germans. Because of them my papa was not here and my mother was always sad. I knew that they were the reason my father had to leave us to fight; leaving us perhaps forever. War had always been a theory, a history lesson. But war had come alive before my eyes. It became personal, and it filled my heart with dread.

I was born into a world on the precipice of disaster. A world filled with suffering and loss. But the world would soon be colored with courage, hope and new beginnings, like mine.

Compassion

On our train ride back to Athens, I stared at a stern-looking Italian solider who sat across from us. I decided I would not let him frighten me so I twisted my face, full of disgust and stuck my tongue out at him. I held on to my mother's leg for protection. He looked at me and shook his head, throwing it back in laughter. My mother's body tensed. I squinted my eyes at him, giving another brave, dirty look. I was not amused that he was still laughing. I was frustrated that I had not been mean enough to scare him. I wanted to be hateful and cruel. My mother looked around nervously as he continued to laugh like a mad man.   We got kicked off the train at the next stop, in the middle of nowhere. We were still many towns away from my mother's *horyo*. The solider uttered a few words in Italian that neither of us could understand, pushing us so hard we almost tumbled to the ground. I did not dare tell my mother. I kept our exchange to myself.

"We are going to have to walk for a few hours," my mother said. She did not know where we were going or which towns were safe. We had no choice, so we started down a long dirt road, passing village after village. My feet grew tired, and my stomach growled with hunger. When I could no longer stand it, I started to sob. My mother gave me both eggs and I practically swallowed them whole. It was too late when I realized guiltily that my mother had eaten nothing.

"But my legs are still tired," I whined. She picked me up and hugged me, managing to carry me for a while. Eventually she had to put me down.

"You have to walk now, Eleni. I don't have the strength anymore," she said breathlessly. As we walked hand in hand, a truck slowed down next to us. My mother inhaled sharply. It was an Italian military vehicle. My mother turned white and froze. I stood at her side, crying. An Italian solider approached. He could not speak Greek, but he motioned with his hands and used facial expressions to form a question that was clear to us: "Where are you going?" My mother used a few words of Italian she had learned since the war began. She understood when he asked her: "*A dove*?" (Where to?)

"Klitora," my mother said.

"*Si.*" (Yes.) He nodded, letting us know he could take us there.

He showed us where to sit in the bed of the truck and covered us with a thick blanket to keep us warm and hide us at the check points. When he offered us water, my mother smiled gratefully, patting him on the arm to express her gratitude. Together we went under the blanket and sat in the darkness. Hours felt like days. As the truck started to make its way down the uneven road, I was hungry again. I began to sob wildly from the pains in my stomach. My mother held me in her arms and smoothed back my hair repeatedly, trying to console me. She sang a lullaby she had sung to me since the day I was born: "Sleep, my darling, while I hush you, and I rock your cradle and I put you to sleep. Sleep, my darling girl, and your luck is serving you, and your good fortune promises you a rich dowry."

I loved my mother's soft song, but it did not help my hunger. I started to feel nauseous because the fumes that came out of the truck had gotten trapped underneath the blanket. Fumes, hunger and the motion of the truck were making me sick. Many times, I swallowed the vomit that came into my mouth. My crying reached a level of complete hysteria. I could not control the screeching noises coming from my mouth and my mother could no longer soothe me with words, promises or songs.

"I am sure *Thea* Maritsa has something warm for you to fill you right back up," she continued. "Please, don't cry anymore. We *have* to be quiet," she pleaded. "When we get home I will make you chicken with lemon potatoes. Just hang on, Eleni. Close your eyes and sleep now..."

The truck slowed down and we heard muffled voices. It was another check point. I could not stop crying and I was only getting louder. *"Please. Stop!"* she hissed angrily. But I could not, would not, stop. Suddenly, a warm stinging sensation spread across my face as my mother's hand struck. In shock, I fell silent. My mother had chased me with a sticks and branches and struck my bare behind with her hand when I was really fresh before. But she had never raised a hand to my face. Because it was dark under our blanket, she had missed most of my cheek and had gotten the side of my nose, hard. Blood ran down my face like a river. She could barely see me in the darkness under the blanket but she felt the blood pool in her hands.

The truck was moving again. We had passed yet another check point. This time, it was my mother who cried hysterically in pain, an awful anguished moan that I had never heard from her before. She held me tight and grabbed the edge of the thick, scratchy wool blanket and pinched my nose with it. It felt coarse and dirty on my little nose. I leaned my head against her chest and her heart was racing.

"It's alright, *Mama*," I tried to tell her between sobs. Tears from her eyes soaked the top of my head. The sting of the slap and blood from my nose was nothing in comparison to what my mother had suffered that moment. In an effort to stop my madness she had gone mad herself. She kissed the top of my head repeatedly and whispered, "I am sorry... I am so sorry... I am sorry... I am so sorry. I love you. Please forgive me... *Please forgive me!*" She rocked me until I fell asleep.

I woke up in my mother's arms and rubbed my eyes. I felt the blanket being lifted and finally took a breath of fresh air.

"Klitora," the solider said, pointing to the sign.

We squinted because the sun was so bright. We had been in the pitch black for only two hours, and the brightness of the sun hurt. We sat up with the blanket off, in the fresh air, as my mother directed him to our home. She offered for the solider to come to our home, that she would pay him with some cheese, bread, whatever he wanted. The solider just smiled and said, "*Anche io ho un bambino a casa.*" (I have a baby, at home.) My mother understood and put her hand to her mouth in sadness and nodded her head in understanding. He turned back to his truck and waved, happy to have helped us.

The Locusts Descend

A locust is the cicada's closest relative. They also come up from the ground. Unlike cicadas, the locusts devour and kill every tree in their path. Like locusts, the Nazis stripped us of our food and left us to die.

Horror

When Hitler's troops came through, they helped further destroy what the Italians had started with machine-like precision. The Greeks had neither the means nor heart to compete in their arena, though many died trying. "Your death is my life," became a common mantra among the Greek citizens. Every death that was not their own, was their own life being spared.

One day, the Nazi flag was raised on top of the Acropolis. The citizens of Athens shook their fists and cried bitter tears every day they looked at it. The most ancient and beautiful symbol of their country, had been tarnished in the cruelest manner. Unlike invaders of the past, the Nazi's did not drop bombs on the acropolis or loot the Parthenon. They were interested in art and architecture and its preservation. Through every beautiful sunrise, sunset, and full moon, the majestic Parthenon remained, untouched. Nazi scientists and architects swarmed around it, taking notes and making observations on the ancient masterpiece.

One night, some young men climbed up, took down the Nazi flag, and replaced it with the Greek one. The Germans were infuriated and appalled that anyone would stand up to their authority. They believed that if they made examples out of young men they accused of this rebellious behavior, it would help deter them. Hangings and shootings of the accused increased throughout the city. This only infuriated the Greeks more, and their will to fight grew stronger.

Cemeteries started to run out of room for the dead, there was no more room to bury them. Much to their surprise, the German's own deaths started to mount rapidly as well. This was unexpected. Even Hitler himself commented in admiration for the Greek soldier's character and he encouraged his own troops to carefully follow the example of the Greek soldier's spirit and dedication. My mother told me how part of this speech had been written in the Greek papers.

Small resistance groups started guerilla fighting throughout Greece and their numbers grew fast. When the German soldiers had a night of heavy drinking, they were picked off one by one as they walked through mountainous regions and they were killed or taken prisoner. Greek women were also strong and committed to helping their men in the army. As winter approached, it was the women who helped clear various mountain passes by hand shoveling and carrying supplies and ammunition to the fighters. They carried at least half their weight on their backs while climbing the icy mountains for miles. One particular group of guerillas took out over seventy German soldiers. The Germans became enraged and went on the hunt for any remaining men. Village after village was raided. If the Germans did not get a satisfactory answer, people were shot or hanged. Entire villages were burnt to the ground. They made their way to a town called Kalavirta, close to where my mother was born. It was December 13, 1943. With *Chrystogena* (Christmas) only twelve days away, it should have been a happy time. Christmas was a time when women were usually busy planning Christmas dinner but some families had no food at all to prepare. Meat was a rarity. The traditional lamb dinner was almost impossible to create. We were lucky, we had lamb to eat.

Outside, the icy snow-capped mountains were beautiful; a stark contrast to the war that engulfed the city beneath them.

My mother and I had gone on another food delivery to Athens, to bring some lamb. As usual, my mother knew we were taking a risk by visiting the city. However, on this particular day, the danger had come to the *horyo* next to ours. The Germans marched into Kalavirta, suspecting they would find the men responsible for the disappearance of their soldiers. Revenge was in order and they already had charged the men of Kalavirta guilty without question. All men twelve years and up were ordered to gather in a field just outside the village for an important meeting. Although the Germans were insistent, their demeanor did not seem violent. They followed the Nazi's like innocent sheep into the open field.

Kalavirta

In this innocent *horyo*, a terrible massacre occurred. I spied on the conversation, as *thea* revealed the horrible details Kalavirta endured that day to my mother. Soula was a cousin of ours who had witnessed the entire event. She had been locked in a schoolhouse which the Germans set on fire.

"They killed all boys…. husbands, fathers, sons in cold blood. I have never heard of anything like it in my entire life," *Thea* Maritsa told my mother, sobbing when we returned. For every German soldier killed or taken prisoner, one-hundred civilians would be executed. This was Nazi law. Tears streamed down her face as they sat down to a cup of thick, grainy coffee.

"I went to see our little cousin Aggelos today before you came back. I don't know if he will make it. He is barely holding on. His mother told me everything that happened. And that your cousin… Michali… is dead," she continued.

My mother gasped, covering her mouth. Tears immediately started to fall down her face. They were as close as Adonis, Vangeli, Yiorgos, Eleni, Thanasi and I.

"Who else?" she asked. My *thea* hesitated for a moment.

"Another cousin of ours, Stelios," she said. My mother and my *thea* sobbed. I was supposed to be asleep. But I was wide awake, holding my breath as I listened to every word.

"Soula told me about the separation of the men and women. How the women clung to their husbands and sons, fearing the worse. Some believed the lie that they just needed to 'talk,' so there was not a lot of hesitation. It would not have mattered. It was an impossible situation. All of those soldiers and their guns; they had no chance. Resistance would have meant certain death. What other choice did a bunch of villagers have other than to believe them and hope for the best? Soula said it was so confusing. They escorted all women and children to the school and locked them inside."

I felt a chill, wrapped up in my warm wool blanket. *Thea's* story scared me. I hugged my knees tight to my chest, in the fetal position. The worst part, I knew, was still yet to come. Soon, I would come to regret my curiosity.

"Soula told me how the elders knew. The looks on their faces made her realize they were all going to die," *Thea* Maritsa said.

Old faces always appeared sour and sad under their deep wrinkles. Their skin looked like brown leather from living and working under the hot sun their entire lives. Of course they knew what the separation of women and men meant. It was a strategy for defeat, one they had seen before.

"Their own parents and grandparents survived through the Turkish occupation. They are the ones who saw it coming," she continued, crying.

I heard my mother's chair move as she got up to hug her sister. I heard footsteps across the kitchen to the *iconostasis*, the central prayer area where our icons are, with candles and incense lit beneath them. My mother kept a candle burning in a small dish of oil in front of our largest icon of the Virgin Mary all of the time. My mother taught me that candles are lit near icons because faith is light. Christ said: I am the light of the world. The light reminds us of the light we all have within, the light in our souls.

"Remember," she explained, "wherever there is light, darkness cannot exist."

The smell of incense wafted upstairs. It relaxed me. I looked above my bed at my own icon of Saint Eleni. I stared at her for a long time. I found it impossible to find peace while we were surrounded by hell.

"I pray for peace all of the time, Maritsa. I pray for my poor Kosta to come back to me. But I don't know anymore how realistic that prayer coming true is... I am sorry. I miss him..." my mother blurted.

"I know. I don't know what to say anymore, to make it alright. Because I know it can't be," *Thea* Maritsa told her.

"It's alright. There is nothing you can do. Stay with me, be my best friend, like always. That is the only thing I need you to do," my mother said.

"Tell me the rest of the story, even though I know how it ends. One day I will want tell it. One day, we will want our stories to live on, even though at this very moment it is hardest to relive them. I need to know."

Thea Maritsa took a deep breath and said, "Once the women were secured in the school house, they were guarded by soldiers. Soula said all of the sudden they saw smoke… then fire. They were planning to burn them alive! They tried to break the windows but they were so thick and they had those iron bars on them…"

My *thea* started to cry as she spoke, causing her to stutter: "But – s-suddenly there w-was a m-m-miracle among the dark chaos. One soldier, with kindness in his soul disobeyed orders. He-he kept looking through the glass on the door but his face, his face… she told me this man was different. He was not cruel or cold like so many of the others. He kept on looking at them, then away, then would pace and wipe his forehead repeatedly. The women knew he was struggling with his assigned task. So they screamed louder, pressing their faces into the windows. He opened the back door, letting everyone escape. The women and children ran for their lives, into the woods and waited for their enemy's departure."

As I laid in bed, I wondered how on this particular day at this particular hour, that soldier who was placed to guard and keep the burning women and children inside felt this great surge of compassion... He could have been stationed anywhere else in the war, but he was there. I realized life is more than luck... God is near. There are miracles, even in the darkness. I felt a flame was lit within me. I would never be able to put it out. There is a reason for everything, even when it does not make sense. This new fire burning in my soul was my belief in fate.

My mother told my *thea*: "One good thing about this war, if there is anything at all, is that we will never take life for granted again. We are survivors and our children and their children and many generations thereafter will admire the strength and resilience that lives in their blood. They are all survivors, too."

"This country and our way of life used to be so simple, so beautiful. It was *ours*. I hope we live long enough to get it back," my *thea* said. Both women sighed simultaneously.

My mother. I loved her so much. I wanted to leap out of bed and hug her. But I know she would punish me if she knew I was still up, listening to all of this.

"The men..." *Thea* continued. "The men in the field were machine-gunned down. Six-hundred ninety-six of them were shot dead. The blood. There was so much, Soula said it ran like a river down the hills. The animals thought it was a stream of water and drank from it."

My stomach turned and I felt like I might be sick. I imagined deer with red lips sprinting across the fields, looking like lions who had just made a kill. I shuttered.

"Thirteen survived somehow and are still under critical care, barely holding on to both life and sanity.... Our little cousin, Aggelos... He told me how they had been instructed to get down on their knees and put their hands on their heads. They were told that this was the pricc for the soldiers they had kidnapped. They had reason to believe the brunt of the resistance was coming from this village. The men of Kalavirta tried to explain they must be mistaken, but the shots rang out with the intention of killing every last man and boy, guilty or not. Aggelos saw his father die. Almost every man that poor boy has ever known is dead.

The women spent hours digging in the frozen ground, to bury the dead. Last night, animals dug them out and this morning, the women put the dirt back on them. The most amazing part is that they do not have shovels. They dig in the cold, frozen ground with their bare hands."

"Maritsa, I know... I know... I hate this war. It's so unfair. God help us. God help us all, not only in Greece but all over this poor world," she said. Both sisters cried.

I felt a lump in my throat and swallowed hard, holding back the tears. I never did well when I heard my mother cry like that, especially since she was usually so strong for me. She reserved tears for the big things. This was one of them. The war had finally broken her down. What if they come here next?

My thoughts were anxious about the next day and the day after that and the day after that... Could something like this happen here?

Of course it could. Horrible nightmares consumed me all night.

Dream

I was running in an open field with my mother, feeling vulnerable, but not sure why. Suddenly, it became clear that we were in danger.

"Run, agapi-mou run!" she screamed.

Bullets buzzed past my ears as we ran hand in hand. No matter how fast our feet tried to move it felt as if we were barley moving. There was no end in sight to the open, vast field. It went on and on, like an endless ocean. Not a home, not a mountain, no other human being in sight. After what seemed like an eternity, we stopped and looked back together because the gunfire had stopped. We sighed in relief. But soon, a different sound frightened us. It was an eerie, heavy breath, accompanied by large steps close behind. A scream tried to escape me, but no sound came. A dark shadow chased us. I knew in my heart that it was some haunted, evil spirit, not a real person. I could not even begin to understand. My mother and I ran fast reciting the Lord's Prayer together: "Our Father who art in heaven, hallowed be Thy name. Thy kingdom come, Thy will be done. On earth as it is in heaven. Give us this day our daily bread and forgive us our trespasses as we forgive those who trespass against us. And lead us not into temptation, but deliver us from evil. Amen." I screamed the words, hoping for the dark thing to disappear.

I woke up. My jaw was sore from being clenched during my nightmare and my forehead was wet. Relief washed over me. It was a beautiful morning, with sun shining through puffy white clouds. As I looked out of my window, I took a deep breath and admired the clouds and the images I saw in them. The smell of the farm, animals and dirt, mingled with blooming jasmine wafted in. All things reminded me that I was safe, and at home. Bells clinked down the road, a man herding sheep. I could almost smell their nasty wool fur caked with dirt and feces. I cringed. Although I loved animals, I did not like dirty, smelly ones.

I headed to the kitchen, excited to go outside and see my cousins.

"Good morning, *Mama!*" I said as I hugged her tightly and kissed her cheek.

"Good morning, Eleni. What can I get you for breakfast?"

"Oh, *Manoula-mou*, can I please eat something later? I *hate* eating right when I wake up, especially breakfast food," I complained.

"Ah, but it is called breakfast because it's the 'break' after the 'fast.' You don't eat all night so you must eat something to stay healthy, keep your energy up so you can play and run all day. It's the most important meal, *kardia-mou*."

"Fine... you are right. I will eat something."

I grabbed a few apricots off the counter, showing my mother with a smile, and ran outside to see what everyone was up to today. She grabbed my arm right as I stepped out the front door. I cringed, knowing what she was going to do before she did it.

She walked me outside and spat on the cement. This custom of my mother's was certainly not shared with any others. It was her special trademark.

"See that?" she said. "I want you to be home before that is dry."

"Yes, *Mama*," I said, rolling my eyes when she turned around. Who in the world could judge the time that would take?

"Don't forget to change before church. There is a special service today. There were some sad things that happened in Kalavirta. I lost my cousin, Michali," she said.

I looked at her frowning and hugged her tightly and kissed her cheeks.

"I am sorry, *Mama*."

"His son Aggelos is seriously wounded but I heard he is doing better today. The doctors think since he survived this long, he will make it."

"How, did they get hurt, *Mama*?" I asked.

"By the Germans, sweetie. They are bad." I looked at her with a face full of worry, trying to hide the fact that I already knew everything. "My love, go and play. There is nothing for you to worry about. Just please be back in time for church."

"Yes, *Mama*," I promised.

Her eyes were bloodshot and tired. My heart sank for her. I wanted to tell her that she did not have to endure the burdens of war alone. She had me. But I could not bear to see her more upset than she already was. She would rather I stay oblivious and innocent, so I would let her believe it for now. She turned from me at the front door and walked to the kitchen table and sat. She picked up her coffee cup, swirling the muddy remains of the unfiltered beans that had turned cold hours ago. I paused at the door.

"Come back in here for a second. Before you go, I want to show you something special that my own *Yiayia* used to do for me," she said. "When I was a little girl she used to be able to see my fortune in the coffee grinds. Let me see if I can tell you yours."

She tipped the cup upside down, placing it on the saucer and tapped on it. She waited a few moments before turning it right side up. She examined the shapes made by coffee running towards the rim. I came closer, sat on her lap and looked, too. It looked like peaks and mountains, but mostly just like a messy cup of old coffee.

"See how this line goes high? You will have a long life. You will have beautiful children, too." I looked at her, waiting for the next prediction. She put the cup down and pushed it away quickly.

"That's all. That's all I can see in there. Such happy things for your future," she said with a forced smile. I smiled and kissed her once again before I ran for the door.

Pausing in the doorway, I asked: "*Mama*, about the spit... Now that I have been sitting here with you for a while –"

"Go. Don't worry about it, please, don't miss church, listen for the bells. One more thing. If you ever see soldiers coming in this *horyo*, run. You run, even without me. Hide and do not come back until they are gone. Do you understand?" she asked.

"I don't want you to worry, I am sure they won't bother our small town. I just want you to know... in case they decide to come here, they are not our friends and you should never go near them," she said.

"Of course, *Mama*."

"Now go ahead and play. I love you." And with that gave her another kiss and I ran off.

That day was like all of the other days my cousins and I spent together. Adonis decided that we would play on the big fig tree in the back yard, a favorite of our parents. It was quite tall and he decided it would be a great one to climb.

"Eleni – you go first. I'll give you a boost," he said.

"Adonis – I am scared my *mama* will slap my ass if I break this tree! And your mother will slap yours too, you know... It is their favorite," I reminded him.

"It's not going to break. I'll show you," he said. He climbed fearlessly to the top. I looked up and suddenly saw him coming down on the branch which bent like rubber. He started to scream. The branch was about to give.

"Ahhhh! You are going to break the tree! Get down from there, stupid!" I screamed.

"I can't. It's bending – I can't get over to the –" *Snap*.

Before I knew it, he was on the ground next to me, along with the fig tree branch. I knew we were dead.

"We broke the tree! My father is going to kill us. Help! Quickly! We've got to get this thing out of here!" he begged.

We managed to drag the branch to the farm next door, tossing it into the pig pen. We hoped the pigs would eat the evidence but we both knew they could never eat all of that.

"Maybe we will get lucky and they won't notice," Adonis said. Suddenly we heard Yiorgos squealing. "*Thea! Mama! Thea! Mama!* Eleni and Adonis did something bad again." For such a scrawny three year old, he had a big mouth.

"He couldn't wait to get us in trouble," Adonis said.

"Come on, *Tzitzika*, let's run!"

We laughed all the way to the olive groves. We were both going to get it later, so might as well enjoy our morning. Up and down the hills and through the trees we wove for hours until we remembered it was time for *Ekklesia* (Church). We ran home as fast as our legs could take us. My mother had asked me not to forget, and I did not want to let her down. After throwing on my dress and shoes, I ran to the church. Church is located, like in most small village towns, in the middle of town, in the *plateia* (square). The bells were ringing as Adonis and I walked into the narthex. I lit a candle and put my index finger, middle finger and thumb to my forehead, chest, left shoulder, then right, the sign of the cross. I leaned over and kissed the icons. I made my way in and found my mother, who was wearing an angry glare. She wrapped her arm around me and I felt her melt. Her eyes were filled with tears. Chanting and prayers started in the sad, solemn atmosphere. I was transported somewhere deep and intensely spiritual.

The Locusts Depart

We lived in the *horyo* for a few more years. Every day we waited for the big disaster; the attack of our homes or news of death. I worried about Germans coming to our *horyo* to shoot or burn us. Awful dreams consumed my nights. I imagined the worst scenario of all, that they would kill my mother and leave me to become an orphan. I wondered and worried about all of these things, playing the different scenarios over and over in my head.

My mother was more nervous than ever. She was bracing herself for the news that my father had died in battle. There had been no news from him or from the army notifying us of his death. Although we tried to remain optimistic, we wondered: *Where did he go?*

My mother feared deep in her heart that the worst happened; lost in battle, his body unrecoverable. So many nights I could hear her, the muffled cries into her pillow. Sometimes I could hear her asking: "Why? Why him? I loved him so much. I was a good wife, I was so good!" She loved my father so. She thought I did not notice whenever she passed their wedding photo on the wall how she touched his face. Many times she would place a kiss on her hand and place it on the photo. It seemed every man except for my father came home from the war. We grieved together because we believed we had lost him. My mother and I started to carry on about our everyday business as best as we could. He never got a proper burial because we had no body. His name was included in a large prayer service for the departed at church. The priest chanted and prayed for his soul. He asked God to give him rest and find a place for him in paradise.

It was as if it were all a strange and awful dream, this vanishing of my father. The last image of him walking away in his uniform will be the last of him I would ever have. His request, "take care of your *mama*," seemed like a heavy responsibility.

When I saw the soldiers who came home embrace their wives and children, I felt bitter at first. I knew my father was never coming home to us, and it made me angry.

Over four-hundred thousand Greeks died and the Jewish community that had lived in Greece was completely exterminated. The economy and infrastructure of Greece was a mess. My mother had to find work or else we too, could starve. She got a job at a small local business that made sweet liquor. The owner provided her with a small supply which she kept at home and promoted the business by serving it to her guests. There was a variety of flavors, including peach, lemon and fig. I was very curious because I heard the adults talk about how flavorful and sweet it was. I hadn't had candy for a long time and was craving something sweet. One day while my mother was at work, my *thea* was watching me. I went back into my house and stood up on a chair to reach the high cabinet where my mother stored the alcohol. The chair was old and the seat was made out of woven straw. I stood up on the tip of my toes and reached for the first bottle I could grab. I heard a crackling noise below my feet and realized the seat of the chair started to give in. With a loud thud I fell straight through the chair, scraping my legs from the bottom to the top on the way down. I had jammed myself into the sharp dry straw.

"Ahhhhhhhhh!" I screamed out loud as the scratches gave way to blood that started to trickle down my legs.

My tears became hysterical between my screams for help. I couldn't get out of the chair on my own, and my legs hurt badly. I knew that my mother was going to kill me for this.

"*Thea! Thea!*" I cried.

She came running with Vangeli in her arms. Immediately she saw what I had been trying to do and shook her head in disapproval. She helped clean me up and closed the cabinet door. She did not tell my mother, but when my mother saw the chair and my legs she knew exactly what I had done. She did not even bother to spank me, I clearly had been hurt enough already.

And so, the months passed much in the same way, one after the other. My mother had worked many small jobs but had not figured how to sustain us permanently. She needed a reliable income so she could plan a future. But how? There was not much work available in the *horyo*. We were already lucky enough to have what we did.

Many were worse off than we were. My entire family planned to go back to Athens when the cooler weather set in. It was decided when the *tzitzikas* stopped singing, we would prepare for the trip home.

One sunny, warm morning at the end of August, my mother and I were outside. She was collecting laundry off the clothesline. There was basil everywhere I looked. It grew at her feet, like weeds, always. She could not get enough of the fresh smell of the herb. She picked a few leaves and smelled them. She ate one, then placed the other in her pocket. Whenever she walked through the room, the fresh aroma of sunshine and basil followed. I watched her as she took a deep breath and closed her eyes, liftig her face to the sun.

Suddenly, *Theo* Stathis ran toward us shouting, "Vasiliki! Vasiliki! Kosta is back! He is walking up the road! He has survived the war! He is *alive!*"

My mother could not seem to bring herself to understand my *theo's* words. She stared at him in confusion. In the distance, a tall figure appeared. My mother blinked her eyes several times as she saw this person approach.

Theo was right. There he was. My *Papa*. He looked different, but it was certainly him. Curious neighbors gathered around the scene with tears in their eyes and hands over their mouths. But it felt like nobody existed except for me, my mother and my father. The air was silent and the presence of him felt surreal.

Was he a ghost? No. He was real; a solid mass of flesh. Until I touched him, I thought he might have been. Although he had grown a long beard, his loving eyes were unmistakable. My father was emaciated; skin hanging off his tired bones. His shoes had holes, toes raw and exposed completely. He was filthy, his uniform shredded; a mere few stitches holding it together. He had an almost lifeless way of moving; an odd shuffling motion, but he had made it. He kept his promise to my mother that day in the kitchen. At first he told her if God was willing he would come back, but my mother made him promise he would come back. To her, God-willing sounded like he had already given up. I was glad my mother made my father's resolution stronger before he left to fight.

My mother steadied herself against the house because her knees had buckled.

"Kirye Elison!" (Lord have Mercy!)

I heard her blurt out as she made the sign of the cross three times over her body, closing and opening her eyes hard and fast. As soon as she re-gained balance, she began to run, tears streaming down her face, to meet him. They hugged each other tight and burst into tears. She took a step back to look at his face, smiling and she lifted her hand to touch his new long beard. She kissed him over and over. Even though I wanted to grab my *Papa* I stood back and gave them this moment alone; the reunion of a husband and wife thought to be separated by death.

"Where have you been? I heard nothing... everyone told me... I believed that you - I thought you were – I thought that you were – *dead*," she told him, crying.

"It was almost true, my sweet Vasiliki. I was close. I promised you both I would come back so I did. But now, it is over," he smiled, staring deeply into her eyes, touching her cheek.

I watched them a few seconds longer until I could no longer fight the urge to run to him. I had to touch him to see that he was real, flesh – not a dream or illusion.

"*Papa*! You are here! I can't believe you are home!" I realized I was screaming the words that came out of my mouth. Then the tears rolled down my face as I broke into uncontrollable sobs.

The three of us stood in a silent embrace. We squeezed each other for a long time. Time stood still and it did not matter what happened around us. My family was together again. It was everything and more a little girl could ever want. In that instant, we were immeasurably wealthy, even if we were a little poor.

My mother took him inside, made him a warm bath and cleaned his body, shaved his face, and made him a meal. She hugged him by the fire that night, rocking him back and forth in her arms just like a baby. I had never seen my father so vulnerable before. My mother nursed him back to health, physically and spiritually. My father succumbed to her care like a wounded puppy, sucking up every tender touch of care like he could not get enough. This day was the first time in my life I realized how much they truly loved one another; it left me awe-struck.

Before bed, I stood at the corner of the hallway clutching my baby doll and stared at them for a long time. Their tender words and touches, the way my mother kissed his head and the way he touched her arm when he spoke to her made my heart warm. *"See that? That is true love, they really are in love,"* I whispered to my baby doll, smiling.

As the days went by and my father started to feel a little better, he told us stories. He spoke of his attempt to return home first. He hitched rides and walked village to village as he traveled. Kind folks offered food and even sometimes a place to sleep. Many of the villages never ran out of food like those in the larger cities did. Most of the soldiers came home this way, through the countryside, and all of the country's people helped them along. He had many thanks and debts to repay.

"I saw where the word *OXI* was carved into the mountain. I bet all the German planes could see it as they flew over. It is beautiful. I will take you both there one day," my father promised us.

My father told me I should be proud to be Greek, that what the Greeks have done in the war is unusual and immense. "Remember, Eleni. We told them 'NO' and we meant it. They could not take our Greece away. Our little country had more passion than two of the most powerful ones in the war. We drove them out. It is so important to remember these days, Eleni, so that you can tell the story to your children and theirs and so on. What a beautiful thing that will be," he said smiling.

"If you tell them all of this, in this way, I will be preserved. All of us will. You will preserve yourself one day too, *Tzitzika*. Like a *tzitzika* who is constantly re-born and rises from the ground, we will rise in a never-ending cycle. If you desire it, you can create it. Future generations will live and feel us in their blood and it will seem almost as if we are alive at the same time together, that in some way, somehow, they know us through a special connection. It is up to you," he explained, with a thoughtful look on his face.

The wisdom of his words and the sweet smell of his pipe infiltrated my senses and made me dizzy. My brilliant, loving *Papa* was alive. My parents had done so much for me. I planned to return the favor and more. *I will tell these stories*, I promised myself.

Although the war was basically over, there were still pockets of guerilla fighting. There were many Germans and Italians who had not made their way out. One night, as we all sat to dinner by candlelight, a knock came at our door. It was a German soldier. My mother tensed, and my father eyed the room, moving swiftly to his gun. The soldier was tear-streaked, crying like a baby.

"Please..." he begged. "Can you show me how to get out of the country? I have been running from my unit for some time and have not been able to get out. They will kill me if they find me, like they've done to all the rest. Can you show me how to pass through the mountains?"

My mother began to open her mouth in protest but my father's look silenced her immediately. "Come, eat. After midnight I will walk with you to show you the way," my father said.

I gulped. Eating was hard. I knew this would put my father in grave danger. There were still guerillas fighting in the mountains, eager to pick off the enemy and now he would be helping one. My father felt pity for the same men who almost killed him and ruined his country. I wondered why. I had never encountered forgiveness of this magnitude until that moment. For the first time in my short life, I realized the depth and beauty of humanity.

My father left with the solider and made it safely back in an hour. Little did we know, that would end up being the last act of heroism he would accomplish in his life.

Back to Athens

We decided to move back to Athens the next week. We took the train with *Theo* Stathis, *Thea* Maritsa and my cousins. My mother explained how everything would become like it was before the war. School would begin, and my father would find a job. I imagined him once again, wearing his freshly pressed suits. He would look happy and handsome and *Mama* would shine his shoes every day.

At first, it was strange to try and forget the last few months of mourning. It would be hard to forget having his funeral service because it was so painful. It would be impossible to forget my mother's muffled cries into her pillow for him every night, asking God why he let this happen. But as more time passed, the bad memories started to fade. My *Papa* was back. Like a *tzitzika*, he rose out of the ground. I thought his body was long gone and I had imagined his bones covered in dust. My father's rebirth was a second chance that we all savored. We loved each other more because we realized the fragility of life.

As soon as we got settled, it became clear that my *Papa* was weak. He was sick all of the time. He was always coming down with one thing or another, and it became impossible for him to work steadily. My mother performed the ritual of giving him vedusas or "cupping" as it has been referred to by many cultures for thousands of years. She took a glass, heated with fire and placed it on his back. The seal created a vacuum. As he leaned over the kitchen chair, my mother slowly moved the glass back and forth across his skin. The suction gave his muscles a deep, warm massage, believed to expel sickness. The thought process behind it was simple: there is a relationship between sickness and pain, stagnation and blockage. The warm process of suction removes toxins, blockages and brings any inflammation to the surface for release, therefore allowing the energy in the body to flow freely. Whether it worked or not, my mother believed it was worth trying. She wanted nothing more than to cure her husband.

He tried to keep his spirits up by spending time with us and with family and friends. The men spoke of many things, but when the topic of war came up, they did not utter a word if women were present. I never heard the horrible things he'd seen, but I could only imagine. His memories gave him a great sense of sadness and anxiety that neither my mother nor I could fix, even with all our love.

"It is a good thing the Friedberg family decided not to return," my father said.

"They would not have made it a day after the Germans retreated," *Theo* Panayotis agreed.

Once I passed by the table of men drinking on my way outside to play. My *Papa* grabbed me by the arm and kissed me on my cheeks then picked me up and placed me on his lap.

"See this beautiful girl, my daughter?" he told them, smiling. "Someday she will have the best. If any man comes to ask for her hand in marriage, I will tell them: show me your bank book first!" he said proudly. "She is my beautiful girl. One day she will have everything she could ever want!" This was my father's prayer for me every day. "My *koukla*," he affectionately called me, smiling and tugging at the two braids in my hair. My uncles and their friends smiled and patted me on the shoulder and I was off and running to find my friends again.

Fighting on the front lines in a horrible war had not killed my father. But the psychological and physical effects were ongoing. He was bitter and scarred inside and out of his frail body. His health deteriorated. One day, the pneumonia came and it settled permanently in his bones. It was the sickest he had ever been by far. My mother kept saying he only needed a little more time to heal, that everything would be fine. But it was not long before his health endangered his life. The coughing was so strong and deep, it hurt my own chest to listen.

"He's coughing up a lot of blood!" I heard my mother's panicked conversation with the doctor. My strong mother had gone to pieces. Did she feel something I did not realize yet? I wondered. Yes, of course she knows. It is death. It is imminent, I realized with a shudder.

The doctor who came to our home told us he was very sorry but my *Papa* was simply too tired, sick and malnourished from the war. He no longer had the strength to fight. He was given days, maybe a week. Death was waiting at our doorstep, for its predetermined collection date and time. The question was, what moment exactly, would death take my father?

His post-war death sentence was far more agonizing than dying in battle. Death should have been quick and easy. I did not want to see him die like this, neither did my mother. He was a soldier and fought so hard for his country. He walked all of the way home from Albania, hundreds of miles, determined to be reunited with us once again. And now we would lose him? It did not make sense. However, he did meet the most important goal he had ever set - coming home to us. Perhaps that is all he had left in him. This final battle he entered, of sickness, he did not have the strength to finish. He could not will his sick body back to health, no matter how he tried. As he lay in bed, I held his cold hand. I kissed and rubbed it.

I was the only one in his room. I wanted to see him alone one last time. "I love you, *Papa*," I whispered. Tears filled my eyes. He lay in such a deep state of unconsciousness. As I stared at his face, I blinked in disbelief when his lips twitched. At first I thought I might have imagined it until he moved his lips again, ever so slightly. I decided this was him trying to smile at me, which lifted my sadness substantially. He knew I loved him, and he smiled for his little girl.

At the exact moment of my father's death, the candle at our *iconostasis* blew out with a *poof*. Suddenly, my mother came charging into his room with the doctor. She saw the candle go out and knew what it meant. Her husband had died. The doctor felt for a pulse on his wrist then listened to his chest with his stethoscope. He shook his head at my mother. She covered her mouth before she cried out: "Kosta! Why? Why? How could you leave me twice? God! Where are you? Tell me! Why? Why does he have to go now?"

She threw herself over his body, sobbing wildly. My *Thea* Maritsa rushed in, removing me immediately, taking me outside where my cousins were playing, oblivious to death. The chaos of my mother's reaction swirled inside of my head and I felt nauseous. My father did not die in battle, but ultimately the war claimed his life.

According to tradition, my mother, aunts and a few close friends helped to prepare his body for burial. All of them were women. I heard some of the words they said from outside as I jumped rope. My cousins asked me what had happened, but I was in a daze.

I never understood how the women could prepare the dead. Many others from the neighborhood poured into our home with food and offered all sorts of help and companionship. It was a shared responsibility. One of the many that Greek women had.

I heard as they prayed: "*You shall sprinkle me with hyssop and I shall be clean. You shall wash me and I shall be whiter than snow.*" They cleansed him in preparation for ascension so he would appear his best at the gates of heaven. This is the reason my mother made me wear my best on Sunday's to church. "Before God, we put on our best inside and out," she told me. I heard everyone inside praying for the forgiveness of his sins, however great or small that were committed in his lifetime, to be forgiven. Incense filled the air as it escaped open windows. I heard the prayers and mournful cries floating up to the sky, and wondered if they'd really reach him, wherever he was. *Did he really already go to heaven and could he see and hear us?* I wondered whether we walked into a beautiful garden or saw nothing but empty black space when our eyes close for the final time. I was not raised to think the latter, but I could not stop my mind from wandering what had happened to him. The questions in my mind would not cease. My poor mother, having to lose him twice. Isn't the death of your beloved once nearly enough to kill you? I thought this might make her angry with God, lose her faith, but I never saw her fall from it. If anything, she held on tighter.

His funeral was small and simple, but the priest's words were intricate and long. The priest said: "Where is now our affection for earthly things? Where is now our gold, and our silver? All is dust, all is ashes, all is shadow…."

My father no longer had the things of this earth, though he never possessed gold or silver. My mother and I were the most precious things lost to him. So why would the priest say this? These words danced around my eardrums and they did not make sense. My mind wandered in the same way it did at school, when the teacher was speaking on a topic that bored me. I have always had a hard time focusing in a teacher to student setting and church sometimes evoked a similar reaction. My eyes glazed over completely. I felt a little guilty about this tendency, but I did not know how to change it. After all, I was just a child.

I stared at the church ceiling. I remember how I used to think the beams that crisscrossed each other all the way up to the top were actually stairs, leading to heaven. I remember being disappointed the day my mother revealed this was not in fact the way.

"But, if these are not the stairs to it, where are they?" I asked.

"God is everywhere. And the best way to heaven is to love. The more you love, the higher you can build your own staircase. You will get there. But not for a very long time," she told me, smiling. "The best way to heaven is through here," she said and placed her hand over my heart.

I tried again to focus on the service. Looking around, I stared at the images of life-size icons on the doors of the altar. If I walked up to the life-size icon of Mary, mother of Jesus, it would be like standing in front of my own mother. I imagined Mary standing next to us, feeling sad for my father, remembering that she lost her boy, too.

The final song of the service began. It gave me chills whenever I heard it, and this time it was even more emotional since it was for my father. The hardest part of dealing with his death was the realization that life would have to go on again, without him. I thought it was interesting and a little sad that for everything that existed, there was an opposite. As I stood at my father's funeral, someone, somewhere, was being born. We would have my father's forty day mass next month and someone that same day might bring a forty day old baby into the church for a blessing, welcoming new life. I thought it was strange, how life and death co-existed. I supposed that God had to balance out the world somehow.

As the congregation sang together, my tears fell fast. I cried uncontrollably, similar to the way I cried with happiness when my father came home to us from the war. Tears of happiness were similar to my tears of sadness, yet the reason for them was very different.

As the last song was sung, I knew this was the last part of our good-bye to him. My poor *Papa*. My poor *Manoula*. I put my hands to my lips and blew a kiss toward his casket. I dropped a rose and a handful of basil that I picked myself, thinking he would like to be reminded in heaven of his love.

I heard the priest chant as he blessed my father's body with incense: "Give rest oh Lord to your departed servant...and appoint for him a place in paradise where the choirs of saints and the just will shine like stars. To your servant who is sleeping now...give rest overlooking their offenses..." Then we all chanted together: "Memory eternal... Memory eternal... May his memory be eternal... Memory eternal..."

I looked into my mother's crystal blue eyes full of tears and held on to her, sobbing. We stood there after each person put a flower on his grave and departed.

I looked through my tears to see Yianni standing in line with a small bunch of white gardenia. He looked at me with solemn face. I mouthed the words without making a sound as the delicate flowers landed in my father's casket:

"Thank you."

I was sure that Yianni had pulled them from his mother's garden and I cringed when I realized he might get into trouble for it. Didn't Yianni know? He was one of my best friends in the world. He could have taken a branch off a dead tree on his way here and it would have meant more to me than all of the flowers that had been given to us that day combined.

Hours felt like minutes. But, finally it was time to go home, get something to eat and rest. We were emotionally drained, as were the ducts in our eyes. There was no more crying to be done that day.

My strong mother. She had the amazing ability through the horror of war and in the death of my father, to make me laugh and feel safe. Many times, I forgot there was a darker side to our lives. In so many ways she made up for the fact I did not have a father, because she was so competent and strong. Her soul grieved in agony over not having her husband and she covered herself in black clothing. So many women suffered the same fate, she was not a lone widow. I never felt that I missed out because I did not get to have my father. I loved him, always missed him, but my mother and I were enough. We had to be, there was no other choice. From that point on, he would have to live in our hearts.

Forty days passed after my father's death quickly. My entire family got together to make *koliva* (a wheat dish offering for departed persons) to bring to church. While the *koliva* was being made, friends and relatives talked about my father. They told stories, cried and prayed together.

As we prepared to make the *koliva*, my mother got her small black tattered prayer book and read out loud: "Christ said, 'Unless a wheat grain falls into the earth and dies, it remains alone; but if it dies, it bears much fruit.' (John 12:24)."

My mother explained to me how and why we made the *koliva*. She told me that all of us must die one day, no matter how sad it was, but that it is also a happy time for our souls, because we rise again and become one with God.

Koliva is made from boiled wheat kernels sweetened with sugar and honey, raisins, cinnamon and other spices, symbolizing that life in heaven is sweet. A mound of it is spread on a platter and covered with white powdered sugar, symbolizing purity. The mound of wheat itself symbolizes a grave. Wheat is used because when a farmer plants his wheat crop, it is buried in the soil, but when the season is right, a new plant will grow, symbolizing the cycle of life. Orthodox Christians believe that when we die, we are raised in a new body, a heavenly one. People, like wheat, must be buried to grow and have new life. Not a new life here, but one with the Lord in Heaven.

When we were finished, we placed a candle in the middle, symbolizing the light of God. We carried it to church and the priest held a special prayer service. My mother told me how it was important to remember and pray for those who have passed on. As Orthodox Christians, we believe that intercessions on behalf of the dead are possible through the fervent prayers from those remaining on earth. I couldn't understand how it happened. All I knew was, I wanted my *Papa* back and it was not possible. My mother's eyes were wet and red as she prayed.

Civil War

On the tail end of the German War, another tragedy began. The Greeks, who invented theater and the concept of tragedy itself, erupted in a dramatic civil war. The war was between the Greek governmental army and the Democratic army of Greece, the military branch of the Greek Communist party. Brothers, fathers, uncles and cousins fought one another based on different political views which had developed strongly through the occupation. Tensions had been forming for years between the leftists and rightists, and exploded once Greece was liberated from the Nazi's.

"This is all we needed. Another war!" my *Theo* Stathis said furiously.

The civil war was not as bad for us as the German occupation and we were not in immediate danger. To be honest, I did not really know much about the civil war because my family was neutral and had not really known anyone from either side well enough to be affected. Many of the guerilla soldiers fought near the mountains and took control over small villages. Countless people suffered greatly, and we were not immune to the fact that once again, war could have made us flee from our home at any moment.

The only person my family had personally witnessed in danger was the old man who lived downstairs from us. He was a known communist. His entire family had been under scrutiny for a while, and he fled to the city, far from his home in the *horyo*, to hide.

The soldiers were exasperated with all of the family members they had interviewed, as they traveled *horyo* to *horyo* in an effort to find him. They interrogated his daughter, a mother of six children, who lived in a remote village. His daughter's family was very poor, and held tight to whatever food supply they could muster. To make things worse, the soldiers constantly raided villages for food. There was almost nothing left, and many people were starving. The guerilla fighters believed they had the right to take food and supplies from the Greek citizens as they pleased. If they were not given what they needed to keep themselves and their men sustained, they would take it with force.

The soldiers went to the communist's daughter's house one day. She had a big dress on and was holding a round belly. But what was under her dress was not a baby. It was their last bit of food, a sack of flour. Without it, her children would suffer, so she held on to it for dear life. She thought this was what they wanted when they knocked on her door and was shocked when they immediately questioned her.

"Is your father the communist?" one solider asked.

"I don't know what you are talking about. I thought you came for food. But as you can see, we have nothing," she told them.

"What group is your father affiliated with? Where is he?" The men demanded. "What village is he living in?"

"He is not here," she told them. They proceeded to raid their home for food and information. Alas, they turned up with nothing. The men were angry.

The mother stood anxiously, waiting for them to leave.

"What are you hiding from us, woman? Here, you have six children and you mean to tell me you have *nothing* to feed them? Your father is a known communist and you know *nothing* about it? We do not believe you!" he hissed.

He grabbed her by the shoulders and shook her.

"My father lives in the city," she told them, crying.

"Where?" the solider asked.

"I don't know, I have not spoken to him in years!" she screamed. It was true. She has been estranged from her father for years. He did not approve of her husband and the poor life he would provide for her. The solider shook her harder. The bag of flour slipped from under her dress to the floor. A white cloud covered everything around them. Her eyes grew wide in fear as they pulled out their guns. She stepped back and told her children to run. But they did not move fast enough and saw their mother killed in front of them. This was ugliness of the civil war that luckily nobody in my family had to witness, the complicated battle whose violence took place on the outskirts of my life. But this story and many like it spread like wildfire. We could only hope it would not reach us. The war lasted less than one year but resulted in so much death. It was not only traumatic because it was yet another war, but also because in this one, Greeks killed each other. They even drafted young girls into their armies and trained them in warfare. Thousands of children were taken from their parents and brought to communist countries to be raised behind the "iron curtain." Some families got their children back, but many never saw them again. For these families, the civil war would never end as they roamed the earth for their beloved children until their death. The thought made me shudder. As the war fizzled, and support from British and Americans stepped in, neutralizing the communist party, the Greek people once again worked on putting their homes and government back together.

Dolphins on Ellas

With my attention focused back on the present, I am at first startled then pleased at what I see. A group of dolphins is swimming alongside our ship. These sweet, happy creatures I have never seen before this moment in my life. They spring out of the water and seem to talk to each other with clicking sounds. They have a calm, wise disposition.

I have only heard of dolphins in myths. I read that they were once human, which is why they are so similar to us. They have been depicted as guides to the underworld because they live between two worlds themselves. They live in the water, but need to breathe air. There are stories of dolphins saving many human lives during shipwrecks at sea, and throughout the times they have symbolized rebirth, mother earth and the human condition. I also once heard a story of a dolphin who loved a human so much that when the human died, the dolphin beached himself to die next to her. I continue to stare at them with wonder.

The Good Years (1946-1949)

I call them that because they were. They were good in so many ways. These years from age twelve to fifteen were the best of my life. After the war was over, there was calmness in the air. War had not been forgotten, but it was like the entire country was able to breathe again, to fill and empty both lungs completely. The warm summer nights returned. When it started to get really hot, the *tzitzikas* buzzed. Steam rolled off the sidewalks and patios when everyone watered them down at night, to cool everything off before sleep. The steam and blooming jasmine smelled like the *kalokeri* (summer) just as I had remembered it. Men would pull out tables and chairs onto the sidewalks, and play long games of cards with cigarettes dangling from their lips and glasses full of *ouzo* (licorice liquor).

The women took the time to clean the house while the children had free reign of the neighborhood. Even though we did not have much, we did not know the difference. My mother would give me some change occasionally to get an ice cream. Every day I was getting older and more independent, and I was so happy, I felt like I had sprouted wings.

I had turned fifteen years old in June. Yianni had a birthday that summer, too. He turned eighteen. Everyone else seemed to know what I kept on denying for so long. He was in love with me. I loved him as a friend, which we had been since we were toddlers. We were like family. But did I love him as a husband? I did not know. I loved him as much as any ill-equipped young girl was able to handle love. I had no experience. When I sensed the intensity of his feelings for me morph into something greater, I did not know how to process it. I was a kid and I wanted to be just that, at least for a while. I was free and life was good. I was too busy living my youth to be troubled with love, even though it was hard, knowing he always wanted more.

Everyone assumed Yianni would get married one day but he would wait a few more years, until I was a little older. His sisters, Athena and Vaso, were also my friends. They showed their approval of me openly. In many ways, they already considered me their sister.

Those days of my life were so beautiful because they were full of innocent love and full of people. I could walk down the street and never be lonely, not even for a moment. There was always someone to talk to, someone to see that knew and cared about you. Nobody was ever alone in my neighborhood, even if they tried to be, it was impossible.

My friend Angeliki constantly pushed boundaries with her parents that I would never dare to. She knew my mother forbade me to wear makeup or wear my hair down. It was against my father's wishes to see me outside of the house without my hair tied up. She had witnessed my mother's crazy spit warning when we asked how long we could go out for. It was so embarrassing. Since Angeliki was older, she thought it would be fun to dress me up in some of her clothes.

"How am I going to get past my mother?" I asked.

"Don't worry, *Tzitzika*. I have a plan. A whole group is meeting here, at my house and we'll all walk together. We'll cover you down the street."

I couldn't help but laugh. She was so fun to be around. She did not have any younger siblings to experiment with like this, so I filled the void for her. She let down my shiny, wavy, honey-colored hair and brushed it.

She wrapped a scarf around my head, which was a combination of black, white, yellow and red, which played off of my skin tone nicely. She gave me one of her shirts and some shoes that had heels. Next, she put a little bit of mascara on my lashes – something I had never even seen done before. She lightly patted my lips with scarlet lipstick so it would not come out too dark.

"Now, brush your lips around each other like this," she showed me, pursing them together, then back and forth.

She brushed my cheeks with pink rouge. Like an artist at her canvas, she took a deep breath and one step back and a smile crossed her lips.

"You look like a *koukla*," she said hugging me tightly. "But wait – there is one more thing I want to do so you will look absolutely perfect," she said. She took out a razor and told me how the style was to have very little eyebrow then you use a brow pencil to fill in a thin, small line.

"Are you sure, Angeliki?" I asked.

"Absolitely, *Tzitzika*. Don't worry, I know exactly what I am doing," she promised.

"Alright, if you think it will look good…do it," I said.

I was excited at what she had done so far, why not add one more beautiful detail? She took some cream and shaved my eyebrows off completely. I gulped. Then she worked with a light-brown colored pencil and drew thin shapes where the hair had been. I looked in the mirror and was pleased. I had sleek, neat eyebrow lines that looked so much nicer than my long messy childish ones. I thought my new look was great, but I knew I had given myself a death sentence. My mother did not even like me to wear my hair down, never mind wear makeup. Even worse, I had no real eyebrows. I knew I would have to fill them in with makeup every day or they would be invisible, and my mother would never agree to that. *I was dead.* This was the only thought I had as I looked into the mirror. *At least I will be a pretty corpse*, I thought. Angeliki grabbed my hand excitedly she pulled me out the door for our ice cream.

"Thank you, Liki," I told her, smiling. I *might as well have fun my last night alive*, I told myself.

Yianni met us at the *kafenion*. That night, in a sudden moment, I looked at him with different eyes. We sat across from one another and I noticed that he was nervous, shaky in his speech and in his hands. He kept looking at me intensely. I wondered if it was my new eyebrows, perhaps they did not look as great as I thought. I started to feel little queasy myself... like a *tzitzika* was fluttering its wings inside of my stomach, I was unsettled. Something was different between us in the instant I walked in with Angeliki's makeover. Maybe it was because he saw me as a woman instead of a little girl, that night. I could not pretend to ignore my feelings as they surged through me as well. *I never had noticed his stubble before... Did his arms and chest look more muscular than usual?* Maybe it was because I looked and felt beautiful that night. Maybe he looked like this for a while, and I never noticed. The only thing I *was* sure of was that I felt awkward and confused. I did not know what to do with my feelings. But I did love the attention from him, the way his eyes locked onto mine. I squirmed nervously, shifting from one side to the other as I bit my lip.

"Eleni, you look so different... You look nice. Not that you don't always look nice..." he stumbled.

I smiled shyly, becoming more self-conscious and insecure in his presence. I took small, careful, spoonfuls of my vanilla ice cream, covered in warm chocolate. Since I was a child, it had always been my favorite, but with Yianni starring at me, I could barley eat it at all.

Rain started to come down heavily as we prepared to go home. Yianni looked at me, took my hand and said: "I'll take you home, Eleni." My finger tips tingled as they found their place around his. *Oh, my mother would kill me if she saw me now.* The make-up and now, *this...*

We ran, stopping under every tree and overhang we could find, plotting the driest path to home together. He held my hand tight in his, never letting go. We stopped again; our faces close and wet. I wondered whether or not my mascara was running down my eyes and if my fake eyebrows had washed off. I slicked back my wet hair with one hand. Yianni gave me a wide smile and he started to lean forward. I turned my head away sharply. Was he going to try and kiss me? Smirking, he put his hand on my shoulder and said, "One more time, let's run!" Oh my God. He *was* trying to kiss me! But our running and laughter dissolved the moment quickly. The rain smelled good. Like something ancient and new at the same time.

"I knew it would rain tonight," Yianni said as we stood under a large tree.

"How, Yianni, are you a magician? There was not a cloud in the sky," I told him.

"You can smell the rain before it comes." Yianni said. "Can't you smell the moisture and see how the wind blows the leaves backwards?"

"No," I laughed.

"Eleni. I am serious. If you would just try a little harder, my city girl, you would be able to see and feel it too."

"Why are you calling me a city girl anyhow? *You* are a city boy!" I said, giggling and punching him playfully in the arm.

"Yes, Eleni, I am. But I take time for nature, to really see it. You get so involved with your girl gossip. You go to the *horyo* every summer but you don't truly *appreciate* what it is you are seeing. Especially lately, with all that dressing up you've been letting Angeliki do to you. You don't need all of this makeup, you know. You are beautiful just as you are. Save your time for admiring the beauty in simple things."

He touched my chin and lifted my face. I felt myself blush and my stomach tingle. If one only pays attention, they can smell an impending storm. But it is our choice whether we listen. Animals don't question it, they always run. They always manage to find a safe place before the bad weather moves in. I wish I knew how to choose simple instinct over complicated thinking. But alas, we are who we are. There is no changing that.

Sorrow and Laughter

On the ship, it is almost time for bed. The sun has set. I reflect on sweet Yianni and how short my teenage years were. It was not enough. There was so much more to learn and say, so much more I had not experienced in life. But America presented herself to me, in all her glory and glamour. It sounded so fancy, so beautiful. But what have I given up for this America? *Everything.* *I have been selfish*, I think to myself. A tear runs down my cold cheek. The vast rocky sea rocks the ship like a mother's hand on a cradle.

Life in America is full of endless hope and the promise of opportunity. I will have riches and a life beyond what I could ever dream of in Greece. *It is the opportunity of a lifetime* - at least that is what I keep on telling myself. George, the handsome Greek-American with chocolate brown eyes and red hair is reserved and quirky, but sweet. I am looking forward to this new adventure, getting to know my husband. But I miss my mother too much already. I long to feel her touch, see her warm blue eyes. Every part of my being is part of her; with every breath I take in, I think of her. I may be a wife but I am also her child. I grieve for my losses: for leaving my homeland, my mother and my childhood behind all at once. But I must be brave, it is all I can do now.

Night has fallen. I stare into the black waves in a trance, pondering the depth of the ocean below me. I wonder what creatures are lurking in the depths that I cannot see. How long would it take for me to reach the bottom? What would happen to me if I jumped right now? My body shudders as a chill runs up my spine. I know I would never do that. I have no wish to end my life. Even though I grew up in a country surrounded by the Aegean, I never learned how to swim. If I found myself in the sea, unquestionably I would drown. I don't even appreciate the beauty of the ocean like other people, who go there to think and relax. The waves have always felt like they were trying to take me with them, like some demonic monster. Anxiety has a voice of its own inside my head. It possesses me uncontrollably, and alters every thought and emotion and it whispers softly: *"Jump, Jump!"* I step backward and gasp. The voice is so clear, so real.

I lick my salty lips. My heart beats loud, hurting my head. My thoughts are so heavy that my shoulders almost cannot bear to carry them. I must have red eyes from all of my crying. I have not seen a mirror in hours, but I do not care.

Why is this voice inside, telling me to jump? I would never do something so dangerous, so idiotic that would hurt me and everyone I love. I am a good wife, a good daughter, I remind myself. What is wrong with me?

I have to get a hold of things. Thank God I have weeks until I arrive in America. Plenty of time left to straighten my thoughts out and clean up the mess that has become me. I shake my head, telling the voice which temporarily possessed me *"No,"* and leave the deck. Once I tuck myself under the cold white sheets I stare into the darkness, hoping for relief, waiting for dreams. But sleep will not come, not tonight.

Friends

As the days passed by, I met three girls, Marina, Afrodite and Christina, all married and older than me. They were all about twice my age, the same as George. They took on the responsibility of looking after me as they would a little sister. We spent many nights talking, laughing and sipping coffee together, listening to music and breathing in the ocean air. Drinking coffee regularly was a new concept for me. But I loved the energy it gave me, jitters and all. We talked about our lives back in Greece and our reasons for coming to America. I did not get into the whole story of how I came to be married, how I had been chosen, just that I had been proposed to by my Greek-American in Greece and now I was moving to be with him and start our life together.

"Eleni – that is incredibly romantic," said Christina through puffs of cigarette smoke, smiling dreamily. She was like a chimney, and I had to try hard to hold back the coughing fits that ensued when the smoke blew in my face. I had never seen a woman smoke like that in my entire life. I felt my cheeks redden, embarrassed that I had not told the whole truth. But the girls did not sense that in me. In their eyes, I was a young love-struck teenage girl.

"Oh, Christina, you made our little girl blush! How cute that she is so young and so in love," chimed in Afrodite. I felt like a liar to them as well to my own beating heart.

I played along, laughing giddily as I continued to sip my coffee.

My favorite type of dance song came on the record we were listening to, *kalamatianos*. Three paces to the right, two the left and then a dip and step back before the line of interlocked hands moved forward again in a snake-like formation. The rhythm of it involuntarily makes my body move in response.

"Girls, shall we dance?" I asked, anxious for a distraction.

"Yes, Eleni – how nice to have you with us, you keep us feeling young!" Christina said, smiling as she took my hand and stood up, snapping her fingers to the music.

We all held hands in a circle and proudly performed the twelve-step dance. Soon others joined in, and some men got down on one knee to clap and whistle for our performance. How Christina managed to keep her cigarette hanging out of her mouth while flinging around a handkerchief in circles as she danced, was beyond me.

We stopped in Naples, Italy before crossing the Atlantic to board additional passengers. My new girlfriends and I were on deck, looking down at a beautiful country quite similar to Greece, the same country that sent my father to war. The similarities between Italy and my Greece made my heart ache and pulse quicken. A small group of Italian soldiers walked past our ship in uniform. I had not seen those uniforms since the war ended years ago, but seeing the soldiers brought back memories, both happy and sad.

Suddenly, as if the crowd was booing a poorly written theatric play, pieces of rotten food and fruit and miscellaneous items started flying off the ship directly at the soldiers.

"Hey Mussolini's! We kicked your butt! Who is the superior culture now?" A group of men chanted together, laughing.

I covered my mouth in shock at first, then I realized all of the Greeks on board were taking great pleasure, so I let myself have a laugh. It was the first time I had laughed that hard in days, maybe weeks. How nice to be able to poke fun at a former enemy and know I was safe in doing so. It was too hard to resist. The soldiers were visibly annoyed but did not even reply, and went on their way. The Greeks took it as a symbol of submission, defeat and reveled in the glory of it. For a little while everyone had forgotten their troubles, including myself. It was a nice change.

Rebirth

A few years after my father died, my mother seemed like she finally started living again, though it seemed she would forever be covered in black clothing. It was another unbearable summer in Athens and we headed for the *horyo*.

"*Mama*, aren't you hot all bundled in black like that? *Papa* would not want to see you in it for this long, and sweltering in the heat like this," I told her.

"Eleni, that is enough. I am a widow," she replied.

When the summer tourists arrived in the *horyo*, the elders sat on their balconies or front steps and watched the younger generations laugh and play, reminiscing about their old days. It was their only form of entertainment in the quiet little town, besides going to church.

Our first morning in the *horyo*, I woke up to the sound of roosters and *tzitzikas* buzzing in the trees. The early buzzing told us the heat would be oppressive. I did not care because I loved to hear them sing.

Every August, we went to the festival of St. Marina. Often, I dreamed of it even during the winter in Athens. It was magical. The church sat perched on top of a high mountain road. It was so crowded that once we got inside, people were shoulder to shoulder. The mass of people stuck together felt like one body. After the service, we headed back down to *plateia*. I was handed sweets by every old *Yiayia* dressed in black with a grey bun in her hair. Old men bearing mustaches and crooked canes gathered in the center of the village to sip black coffee, smoke and have meaningful, passionate conversations and debates. A band played and we danced all night. I closed my eyes and brought my arms up, snapping my fingers, twirling and singing. I danced. And I danced. Women came, arms full of homemade bread and sweets. Lamb sizzled on the fire and we ate and ate until we had to dance it off again. It was beautiful.

A Cicada's Vulnerability

A cicada's most vulnerable time in their lives is right after they come up from the ground, still in their childhood stage. They immediately shed their outer layer of skin when they are still low on the trunk of the tree. Having just shed, they need rest before climbing high up in the leaves of trees for safety. This is when they are in the greatest danger, when the birds can easily pick them off.

The Meeting

The air had grown cool and silent once again, and the *tzitzikas* moved underground. My mother and I headed back to the city. Home. I was excited to see all of my other family and friends who had either stayed or gone to other villages for heat escape vacations. I skipped into my city, looking for all of the familiar faces. Yianni was the first person I saw.

"We're back! I don't have time to talk about my trip now, Yianni. I am running over to my *Thea* Maritsa's house with my mother." I gave him a quick hug and ran off, waving. I ran to catch up with my mother who hadn't seen my *Thea* Maritsa for weeks. As usual, the two sisters were dying to talk about anything and everything.

"I'll catch up with you later, Yianni," I said looking back as my mother dragged me quickly along. I smiled and waved. The special way about him that was purely Yianni made me happy. I always felt home when I was near him. His eyes that danced when they were fixed upon me were almond brown and reminded me of chocolate. Sometimes he did a strange thing when he looked at me; he looked at me and away a few times as quickly as you would blink your eyes. It was like he second guessed who he saw in front of him. It was strange and comforting at the same time. His hair was black and smooth and a touch of wild. All of his wonderfulness was within my grasp if I had only wanted it. If I only confirmed what he had been waiting for. I did not react to his words or advances concerning us. Most of the time I would laugh, change the subject, acting like we were best friends and nothing more. Sometimes he would hang his head in defeat. How I wanted to put my hand to his cheek, but I would not want to let us get that close. I knew he would have taken the perfect opportunity to touch my face and then we would kiss. Kissing him is something I have tried to avoid many times. Why was I scared of kissing him? What was my fear of committing to such a perfect person? Was I just too young? Would our love grow in time? Or would I always feel this emotion I could not seem to label? Indifference? That is as close as I could get, but the word seems too cruel a definition.

When my mother and I arrived at my *thea's* house, I sprang into her home shouting, singing and dancing.

"Hi *Thea*, we're back!" I exclaimed, twirling into her house, creating my own little routine as I danced along, kissed her on both cheeks and gave her a warm hug. I will never forget the next moment. I caught my reflection in the mirror of the adjacent room and noticed someone else was also in it. A man, whom I had never met, stood meticulously combing his red-colored hair. He stopped abruptly and stared. He was very good-looking, tall with deep, dark eyes. The expression he wore was serious, almost a scowl. I gasped after my body realized it had forgotten to breathe for a few moments. He took a sudden deep breath as well, eyes fixed on mine. Everything was moving slow as a strange feeling engulfed me, a sense of danger which I could not explain. I pushed away the feeling, laughing inside at myself for being awkward and paranoid.

"Eleni, *koukla*, this is my sister-in-law's nephew, George, from America. He is getting married in two weeks. He has come to meet his bride," my *thea* explained.

"Nice to meet you," he said. He moved toward me and took my hand in one smooth motion.

"Nice to meet you, too," I replied, trying to swallow the lump that had suddenly formed in my throat.

He spoke Greek with a funny American accent.

"He is going to be married to a beautiful girl from the island of Kos in two weeks, aren't you, George?" *Thea* said, moving close to him and nudging his side with her elbow, reminding him. He did not acknowledge my *thea's* words. He was busy staring at me. My cheeks grew hot.

There was a look between my mother and my *thea*, an unspoken language only sisters know. Disapproval. My mother cleared her throat and said good-byes quickly. I left my *thea's* house deep in thought about the mysterious red-headed man and the country he came from.

America. I had never met nor ever spoke to anyone who lived there before. How lucky is that girl he is going to marry? He will take her to America with him! In America, anything you dream of can be yours – jobs, money, big cars and homes. America was an unreachable place I would never have other than in my daydreams.

Wanted

I left my *thea's* house in awe. As I walked beside my mother, my imagination ran wild. I entered a day dream about what it might be like to live there myself.

"Oh, Mrs. Eleni – how nice to see you," the boutique owner would say. I would buy beautiful clothes and accessories and I would go home in my shiny, new, big car to my big house.

"My beautiful wife, how are you today? Did you buy all of the nice things you needed and wanted my dear?" my loving husband would ask.

Then he would smile and kiss me and my kids would laugh, jumping around and in between us. My children would be well dressed and in possession of everything they needed and wanted. If there were no financial worries like we had in Greece, maybe people have only room for happiness and peace... what a happy dream. This is what I believed people lived like in America.

"Eleni, you are going to walk into that street lamp if you don't wake up! What on earth are you thinking about?" my mother asked, startling me.

"Oh – nothing Mama just a little tired, that's all," I said, rubbing my eyes and forcing a yawn to convince her.

In the minutes following our departure from my *thea's* house, I had no idea what transpired as the door closed behind me. A single moment, a chance meeting, had changed everything. That moment was all it took to forever change the direction of my life, and I did not even know it yet.

George confided to my *thea* he no longer wanted to marry the girl from Kos. He wanted me for his bride instead. He did not even want to meet his fiancée in person, to be sure. Even though she tried to persuade him that it would cause his parents great embarrassment, he did not seem to care. I was sixteen, he was thirty-two, but he told her that he did not see that as a problem either.

My *thea's* attempts were useless. She may have well been speaking to herself. Nothing could curb this new appetite he developed. He was intense, determined and did not take advice from anyone. His passions were set. He could not eat, sleep or do anything but think of how much he wanted me while I lived my normal day to day life, oblivious.

It seemed that everyone else knew George wanted to marry me before I did. George spoke to my mother and my uncles. *Theo* Stathis and *Theo* Panayotis told my mother to hold her tongue and to let me leave if I wanted to. They believed going to America was the best chance anyone in our family would ever get. And so, my mother, uncles and aunts called a family meeting, to discuss the biggest decision I would ever have to make in my life. As I took in their words, their recommendations, their insistence that this was all up to me... I did not know what to think. I reflected on the daydream I had when I skipped back from my *Thea's* house after meeting George. The dream... I could live it every day for the rest of my life. I dreamed of it, and then there it was, right before me. I became excited about the prospect of going to America.

I was caught up in a storm of negotiations. My head swirled. I said yes to George's proposal. However, my excitement quickly became tinted with nervousness when the reality of leaving my mother sank in. One of the terms of our marriage, the promise George made to my mother, was that we would send for her papers as soon as we got settled and she would come live with us.

Soon, everyone in the neighborhood seemed to whisper when I was near. I could see looks and hear hushed voices everywhere I turned. I knew nothing of this girl he was promised to in Kos, and even though I tried not to, all I could think of was how awful she must have felt. To be promised to a handsome American then have him change his mind less than two weeks before the wedding must have been horrible. In one instant her entire future was taken away, her dreams of escaping to America smothered. In one instant, one chance meeting, I became the lucky one. If I had not been back from the *horyo* that day or at my *thea's* house that hour, everything would be as it always had been.

I never had the urge to live a different life than what I had, with my mother and my family so close. It was a beautiful life. But, after meeting this American, leaving was all I could think about.

Accepting the proposal was my decision alone. My mother did not try to convince me either way, but was upset I would be moving so far away. My *Theo* Stathis and *Theo* Panayotis stayed by her side and kept encouraging her to be happy, that this window of opportunity would be good for the entire family. My mother was in more agony than she ever let on.

I would marry this stranger named George in less than two weeks. It had to happen so fast, I was lucky to have found a dress in time. My mother did not get too enthusiastic, but nor did she reveal her pain, even though her world was collapsing. She had no husband, one child and I was leaving. She was about to lose everything.

Confrontation

Overnight, I gained the status of a movie star. For a brief moment, I loved the feeling but my heart sank as I realized Yianni would soon find out. All of my glory faded and my heart ached because I had to tell him, if he didn't know already. At minimum, I owed him an explanation. I knew he would try to talk me out of it, and I was afraid to face him with my decision more than anyone else.

As I walked home from visiting my cousin Eleni, Yianni caught me off-guard when he jumped out of the shadows on my street. My breath caught.

"Yianni. You scared the hell out of me! How are you?" I smiled. *Does he know?* I wondered.

"Eleni," I heard his whisper and walked towards him. He was tear-streaked. *Of course he knows.*

A lump formed in my throat that I could not swallow. His hair was disheveled, a long strand glued to the side of his face. His clothes were a mess. It was odd to see him this way. This year, he had become a member of the Greek Navy and was usually the put-together type even when not in uniform.

"I did not think I would have another chance... to see you again before... before... So. Tell me. How soon is it anyway?"

My stomach dropped. A horrible feeling came over me. I was a horrible person because I had hurt him. I felt guilty that I never felt the emotional attachment to him relationship-wise that he clearly had for me. I wish I had. However superficial, at this moment, my anticipation of living my life in America was stronger than any feelings I may have had for

Yianni. I did not feel ashamed for wanting a good life, only sad I had hurt him.

"Two weeks," I said.

"Yianni, this will be good for me. This is - a good thing."

Words rolled off my tongue like lead, hard and heavy. I felt confused as my head spun and my heartbeat quickened. I was *torn*. What was happening to me? I could not believe my own mind and heart. It became hard to look him in the eyes. My smile became so forced, that my lips shook in rebellion. I trembled. He moved closer to where I stood.

"You don't even know what America will be like. What if all you hear about how great things turn out to be exaggerations? What if he is not good to you? He does not even know you. How could you be sure he would love you the way I do..." his voice trailed off, half regretting his admission. It was now or never. He ran his fingers through his hair, half covering his eyes and hanging his head down away from me. This was the first time he proclaimed it out loud. I felt an uncomfortable shift in the air between us. Feeling and thinking he loved me was different than actually hearing it. His words felt like a slap in the face; a harsh reality I did not want to know. I had my plans, I would not change them now. I would lose everything I had ever dreamed of having in life. I stood there immobile, frozen, cold as a stone, debating my next move, struggling for words.

I felt three things at the same time: I obviously had feelings for Yianni, which stirred in that very moment he stood, tormented, before me. I had never admitted love for him before, but the feelings I felt were surely real. I grew desperately sad about my decision to close the door to having him in my life forever.

Second, it was hard to conceal the excitement I felt about starting my new life with a handsome husband in a new and exciting place – America. It was everything I ever wanted and more.

Third, part of me was angry with Yianni for trying to stop me, for making me feel torn up inside. Why did he even have to tell me that he loved me? What was the point? I would much rather have had him let me go without a word, even hide his feelings for my sake.

My departure was already painful in leaving my mother and family, but with Yianni's added profession of love, it was all too much to take. I would certainly sacrifice my sanity, though, if telling me he loved me made his life more manageable, a life without regret. He will always know he tried, and it was better for him this way instead of never being able to forgive himself for things left unsaid and undone.

"And what about your mother?" he asked. "You are going to leave her? She has no other children, she lost your father. Are you sure she will be alright?"

If I stayed here, loved Yianni back and ended up marrying him, I could be happy. I would be with my mother, all of my cousins, aunts and uncles for the rest of my life.

I had never thought about the consequences of my current choice versus life with Yianni before. I knew my mother would come one day, when we got her papers. *But how? When? How long would it take? What if I could not get her to America at all, ever?*

Yianni, who came out of the shadows to tell me that he loved me that night, made me feel like my world had been turned upside down. My dreams and hopes for the future had kept me from seeing the reality of it all, the consequences of my choice. The tears on his sweet face were real and plentiful and all for me. This life is real; life in America is a dream. Yianni is my friend, he loves me. George is a stranger. As I look at Yianni's tears fall, I realize I have never seen anyone cry like this because of me. The biggest decision of my life, I had made too quickly.

"Just give me some time," he pleaded.

"Give me time to show you how much I care. How we could be happy together, here, now, forever. I would work hard, provide you with everything you need. Run away with me now. We can elope. Run away with me now, please Eleni. You don't have to get married and move away from your family to have a good life. I will love you unconditionally. I promise. Just give me some time. I will make a life for us. I will always love you and do everything for you."

He stepped forward and held my hand in his. I shivered as the hair on my arms stood up straight.

His words meant more to me than George's proposal. The proposal, which had consisted of discussions between my mother, aunts, uncles and George never once mentioned *love*. I nodded my head in agreement, too excited for America to think everything through slowly. The sweetest thing George said was after I accepted:

"I really like you. You are perfect for me."

I really like you? Why didn't I run away at *that* moment?

George might think I am perfect for him. *But who is perfect for me?* George *likes* me. Yianni *loves* me. But I had made my decision, and felt it was too late.

"Yianni… I am so sorry. I just – I don't – I mean – I just don't feel the same way! I can't give you more time… because I don't have it!" I blurted and pulled back my hand from his.

My body twitched involuntarily when I heard a voice inside me yell *"you're wrong!"* But I ignored it. I was lying to myself, and I knew it, I just wouldn't listen.

He turned the other way, unable to look at me. He bent forward as if my words had physically come out of my mouth and punched him in the stomach. When he regained composure he turned to face me. He stood so close his breath blew my wisps of hair aside.

"You have always been a stubborn girl. I know that no one can change your mind once it is made up. I should have known better. I should have asked your mother for your hand earlier…" He cracked a slight smile at me. "I wanted to last year. But you were so young, we both were. You still are, you know…"

He took one finger to my chin and tilted my face up to his. My breathing ceased and my stomach lurched. I stood in front of him, looking up, speechless. Suddenly, his lips were on mine. I did not react. I wanted to kiss him back. His kiss was so warm and sweet and it was my first kiss ever. I was resisting because of my decision, my new role as a fiancée. Since I did not kiss him back I could justify this entire situation with the simple fact: he kissed me. I would remain a proper lady who is engaged to be married.

I gently placed my hand on his chest and stepped back. "I should go." I took a deep breath and gave him a hug, inhaling his scent for the last time.

I had to go, fast. I could not start to meddle with fate now. My new life was hanging in the balance and I could not ruin it. I turned my head in the direction of home, ready to say good-bye.

"Wait. I have something for you. I made it myself."

His father was a jeweler and he was his apprentice. He pulled out a thick gold band with an "E" engraved on it. Intricate designs surrounded my initial. It reminded me of palm trees. It reminded me of Greece.

"Yianni, this is beautiful. But you didn't have to. I mean – I don't even know if this is approp– I can't – shouldn't take –" I choked on every word.

I wanted the ring because it was so beautiful, but at the same time I didn't want it. To carry the burden of the pain I have caused, permanently. Set in gold. It will haunt me, follow me forever.

"Shhh… Please just take it. A gift. From me. I made it myself, and it's only for you. It is no good to anyone else. It's personalized. You don't have to tell *him* or anyone who gave it to you."

"I will never have you. But we will always have… this," he said.

I knew what he meant by *this*. A blossoming love that would never come to fruition. His honesty made me dizzy. We would always have a beginning and no end. A beautiful tree full of buds about to bloom that gets its branch snapped off. The damaged tree still lived on. If Yianni and I were a season it would be summer; hot, bright and young. I felt so nervous, beads of sweat started to form under my arms.

My mind flashed back to us as children holding hands, laughing and running free together. With a heavy heart I tried to catch my breath. I stumbled to find the right words as my mouth went dry. I knew I had to compose myself before I fell to pieces.

"Thank you. I love it, really. I do." It was so ornate and intricate; I could only imagine how many hours it took his hands to make it, how many times he must have burned his fingertips with melted gold. For me. When I slipped the ring on to my index finger, it fit perfectly. Of course it did. He had always paid so much attention to me. He even knew the exact size of my finger. I closed my hand into a fist around it in an act of protection, to protect this precious gift in a way I could never hold or protect him in this life. All I have ever done is hurt him.

"Let me see," he said, as he took my hand in his. My fingers tingled at his touch as he wrapped his fingers around mine. I was taken aback by the intensity. Just then I heard my mother's voice. She was looking for me.

"I'll be right there, *Mama*."

"I have to go," I said, slipping my hand out of his.

I saw the shadow of my mother at the front door. She strained to see who I was speaking with. "In case I don't see you…" he started.

"Of course you will. When have I ever gone two weeks without seeing you, other than when I went to the *horyo* with my mother?" I said, laughing and casually nudging his arm.

"I know, but this is different, Eleni. And now you have to spend time getting to know your – your. *Future husband,*" he said through clenched teeth. He inhaled sharply.

"Yianni, please. I will see you. Don't do this," I begged.

"I won't see you again, Eleni. I know I won't. Just to see you tonight was difficult enough, your uncles have been watching my every move so that we wouldn't get a chance to see each other."

I laughed. "Don't be silly, Yianni," I told him, even though I knew it was the truth. "Yianni. Come to my wedding, please. It won't be the same without you," I said.

"I don't think you would want me there, Eleni. I will not wish you luck and happiness like some phony when all I want is you for me."

I could feel my emotions about to spiral out of control. "Good-bye Yianni," I blurted. I turned to run, but his strong, calloused hands grabbed my shoulders and turned me towards him. We stood face to face.

"I have one thing left to say before you go. If you change your mind, I will be here... waiting. You can always be sure I will be here and I will love you. That will never change. Always. Wherever I am, whatever I do, if you come back to Greece I would leave it all for you, I promise. That is, of course, if you wanted me..."

I swallowed hard. What did he say? Why did he say it? I was flattered, surprised and sickened all at the same time. How could he say these things so confidently? Nobody knew how they would feel in the future. *Right*?

"I love you. I wish you felt the same, and that we would not be saying good-bye like this. But if you realize you feel the same too, before you get married, come find me. I will be nearby until I see you come out of that church married. After the church bells ring, and the rice is thrown, I will disappear for good. After all, I only want you to make the choice that makes you happy."

There was nothing for me to say, because I could not find the words. Tears ran down my face as I held up the ring, whispering "thank you" between sobs. I turned around and ran home as fast as I could, crying, without looking back. The only sound was my heart beating and my feet hitting the street. I was only five houses away from mine but it felt like miles. My lips still tingled from his kiss. I heard an anguished moan, and I felt like the ground had dropped from beneath me. *What have I done?*

I stood outside in the front of my house for a moment. I did not want to let my mother see me like this.

She peeked her head out the front door again.

"Eleni, are you coming in now?" she asked.

I wiped my tears with the sleeve of my shirt.

"I am just going to pick some basil, *Mama*," I said. I came up with the lie quickly. It made no sense why I was picking basil in the middle of the night, but my *mama* did not seem to find it odd. Her emotions and thoughts were also in a distant, painful place.

I picked a handful of basil and breathed it in. I looked at the red dahlias in my mother's flower bed, which she had planted with such care. Everything she touched bloomed. This little yard in the city is where I learned to walk and run, where I played with my mother, father, cousins and friends for hours. I bent down and took a fist full of dirt in my hand and squeezed it, letting it all slip between my fingers back onto the ground. *Good-bye*. I whisper. *Good-bye home. Good-bye Papa, wherever you are.* I stood up and looked at the sky and wondered if he was looking down at me.

My father's grave was a short walk from my house. I found myself running towards it as my legs moved before my mind. I needed to see him one last time. When I arrived, I collapsed onto my knees, crying and stroking his name etched in stone. *Kostandino*.

"*Papa*. I need your help. I hurt. Yianni hurts. *Mama* hurts. Everything hurts. What do I do, *Papa*? What did I do? I need a sign… please… just some guidance… *anything!*"

I pleaded for an answer and waited on my knees. Unaware of how long I was there for, when I finally got up and my feet were numb. My father gave me nothing despite my desperation. He was gone. I could not feel his presence. Just like when we thought he died in the war all traces of him had vanished from my world, and the pain of losing him hit me all over again. I could not help but wonder eight years later whether or not heaven was real. As I walked up toward the door to my home, a loud crunch beneath my left foot made me look down. It was a cicada. A hoarse scream escaped my lips. I didn't know what it was doing on the ground, or around at all, but I killed it. Or was it already dead and fell from the tree? It must have been the last one of this summer. *Is that your sign, Papa? A crushed tzitzika? What in the world does that mean?* I started to cry all over again.

I wiped my eyes as I walked through the door. I forgot the basil somewhere, but my mother did not notice.

I made my choice and Yianni couldn't change it; my love for my mother would not change it either. I was determined. Both Yianni and my mother knew this about me. They both knew I would go through with this. I gave my mother a hug and a kiss and told her I was tired. I was too drained to cry again. I had no energy left. My head hit the pillow and my eyes were heavy. I prayed for Yianni. I asked God to make him happy, give him a wonderful wife. Give him the things I never could. I prayed for God to forgive me if this decision was selfish, to ease my mother's pain while we were apart. I told God he had permission to punish me for hurting Yianni like this. Whatever was coming to me for breaking his heart, I decided, I was ready for. I deserved it. When sleep finally came, I was tormented by nightmares.

Train Wrecked (Dream)

I found myself in a panic at a small train station. I sensed immediately Yianni was near. I looked down and saw him laying on the tracks. As I approached, he looked right into my eyes, helpless. He was dirty, his clothes were ripped and he was bleeding. "Eleni... I love you." he said in a whisper that was barely audible. "I am dying... it is time for me to go now...." I fell to my knees on the ground beside him. His body looked broken and he was bleeding heavily from his chest. "My chest. It hurts. The first train punctured my heart... I know I don't have long now."

"The first train? What do you mean, first train? What happened to you?" I asked frantically. I took him in my arms, not believing he could die and rocked him back and forth. "Yianni, please don't go. Don't!" I looked up and screamed for

help between my sobs. The station was empty. It was as if everyone disappeared.

He made an effort to speak again but this time I could not read his lips. It was as though he was speaking a foreign language I could not decipher. My soul could hardly bear the pain. He was dying and it was my fault. If I hadn't broken his heart, then maybe he wouldn't have been upset and fallen in front of the train.

"My God. Yianni. Did I do this to you? Did I make you jump in front of this train?" I asked.

"Can't you see, Tzitzika?" he asked.

I could barely see his face through my tears. "You are not trying hard enough, Tzitzika. To sense the storm...You know what I mean but you will never admit it to yourself. It is not me that is in trouble, it is you. You will never sense the rain before it comes."

"Yianni. I don't understand. You are delirious. Help! Somebody please help us!" I took my jacket off and pressed it hard on his chest in an effort to stop the bleeding. Soon it was soaked red. I screamed at the sight of so much blood spilling from his body.

Just then I saw my husband-to-be George, walking on the other side of the tracks, smirking at us then continuing on his way. "George? Is that you? George, help please! Help us!" I screamed. But he did not look concerned. He stared at the both of us coldly and turned away. Once he was gone, I heard the sound of eerie laughter in the distance. Yianni started to close his eyes, and I was in complete panic. I cried and screamed with such force, it physically hurt. My throat burned and my voice was fading quickly from all of my screaming. He is going to die! The realization filled me with more horror than I had ever known.

Something landed on my shoulder, I turned to look. It was a cicada, and it began to sing. At first I smiled. It was a little strange but pretty. Cicadas don't bite but they do have a long nose they bury into tree branches in order to eat what is inside. They rarely mistake people or other animals for trees. Just as I processed that thought, I winced in pain. To this particular cicada, I was a tree. I flailed wildly in an effort to get the thing off, but the cicada was unaffected. I felt it pierce through my skin and suck my blood with stabbing pain. As I screamed out, I arched my back and looked up at the sky. "Papa!" I screamed towards heaven. I looked down at Yianni, lifeless in my arms.

When I opened my eyes, I was panting, sweating and crying hysterically. For a moment, I did not know whether the dream I had was real or not. The depth of what I had done to him startled me, the fear and urgency in Yianni's voice broke my own heart into pieces. "You are the one in trouble."

I wondered if my screams reached my mother's room. She had not come in to check on me, so hopefully she did not notice. My throat burned as if it had been engulfed in flames the entire night. I am not sure how I had not roused her from her sleep. She would certainly want to know what it was that I had been dreaming about. It was so real, I thought as I pinched myself and took a deep breath.

Women in my family have always dreamed vividly. Some days my mother would warn me to be extra careful, not go or to go somewhere, go tell someone something all based on an obscure dream. There are old *Yiayia* tales in our family about certain types of dreams. For example, if you dream of fish or dirty water there was something terrible about to happen. Why a fish? I often wondered. Perhaps it was a bad omen because a fish, dead or alive, in murky water brings an unpleasant odor to the senses. Distinct smells stay imprinted on our memories far longer than any other sensory experience.

One thing I knew for sure; I could not allow myself to run into Yianni again. I would only cause him more pain and I could not bear to do that. I decided that if I caught a glimpse of him near the church I, would pretend not to see him. I had to do that. I needed to hide my guilt and tears and move on with my life. I had to try to never wonder what could have been with him and concentrate on the present. Yianni was the first heartbreaking decision I ever made about love. This wound would leave a scar; spoil my innocent heart in a way that could never be mended. First loves do that.

My mother told me once that sometimes glass breaks and you might try to fix it. But no matter how hard you try to put it back together, the cracks would always be visible. We could try our best to mend our hearts when they break, but we would never see them again in their original condition. I bet my mother's heart cracked when my father died. My heart broke over Yianni. The tiny fissures grew with every breath. Would it crack enough to shatter completely and destroy my whole heart or would I be able to mend it enough?

A Cicada's Adult Life

A female cicada finds her mate and sings. She sings with her wings flapping high in the treetops all summer long. Cicadas only have the summer, a single short season to live. In the end, this is what every species has, one chance. One choice. She will lay her eggs and die. And the cycle continues. Life will go on without her.

Courting

The date was set for the last week in September; I had chosen my mate, my husband. Arranging for his parents and my mother to meet on the phone would be the only introduction our families would have before our marriage. My mother did not have a lot of money to offer, but promised to send me with a trunk full of dowry. Linens, silverware, bedding, curtains, quilts and crocheted doilies (many of which my mother and I made together) for decorating. My mother promised to put together everything I needed. It felt like a business exchange took place.

My wedding. It was going to happen in two weeks. The same exact day he had promised to wed another. Part of me still felt badly for the girl I didn't know, George's would-be bride.

My cousin Eleni chaperoned some of our dates. One night, George decided to take us to a movie. I was excited. I hardly ever got the chance to go to the movies, and I was so happy my cousin would be there with me. It was an American movie, and I was excited to sample the flavor of the land I would sail to soon. We walked along, enjoying casual conversation on the cool, crisp September night.

Out of the corner of my eye, I saw Yianni. Immediately I could tell he was surprised, and he seemed to lose his equilibrium as he walked down the street. He almost stumbled when his eyes met mine for a brief moment. Feeling flushed, I turned away, acting nonchalant. Inside, my stomach was in knots. As we got closer, he simply stopped and stared. I could feel his eyes burn through me. I kept myself together on the outside and kept walking without giving him recognition. I knew I was behaving terribly, acting like he was a stranger on the street, but I did not dare speak to him in front of George. *God. Why did I keep making bad things worse?* I began to think perhaps I found my niche in life – creating disasters.

My cousin Eleni was busy telling stories about our youth to George. Neither of them had even noticed Yianni. I laughed along, nervous, and half listening until Yianni was out of view. I took a deep breath and tuned myself back into the conversation.

"And then, one time when our mother's gave us money to get an ice cream, your future wife here, (whom we should have nicknamed Clumsy instead of *Tzitzika*)... was laughing and joking around. She was so busy laughing, that she smacked into a street sign straight on in the face and smashed her ice cream in it. Oh, and let's not forget the time you fell into the sewer?" she added, laughing. "We had fun, didn't we, *Tzitzika*?"

"Sounds like I am in trouble," George said, lips forming the closest to a smile I have seen yet.

"Oh, come on, Eleni, I did those things to make everyone laugh," I argued, slightly embarrassed.

George made no comment and did not look at us as he walked ahead. As my cousin and I gleefully approached the theater, arm in arm, we smiled excitedly and looked at George to purchase our tickets. He looked at the both of us as his expression turned into a scowl.

"You know what girls - I don't feel like going anymore. We're not going to the movies tonight. I have changed my mind." And with that he turned around and started walking.

Eleni and I looked at one another in bewilderment. I did not understand. Had I done something wrong? Made him angry? Did something about the stories we shared aggravate him, change his opinion of me?

Oh God. I had definitely done something. Maybe he was mad, maybe he thought I was a stupid blonde, no brains. Why did my cousin have to tell all of those stupid stories about me? She made me look like a child. No man wants a child for a wife. Something had gone wrong. I was not the lady he expected. I tried to blink away the tears that stung my eyes.

George turned around and motioned to us impatiently with his hands to follow him. Not a word passed his lips. He walked far in front, anxious to get us home. He was so far ahead, it didn't even seem like we were even out together.

Eleni held my arm tight and whispered: "His mood changed completely. Just like that.

It doesn't make sense. I am confused. Have you seen him do this before? Is he always this serious?"

She asked me question after question that I didn't know how to answer. "I don't know, Eleni. I mean, I haven't seen him do anything exactly like that before. Maybe he doesn't feel well and was too embarrassed to tell us about it?" I hoped my theory was true. If it wasn't, I had nothing. I had no idea what was going on with him. I could not understand. I saw the worry in my cousin's eyes. Should I have asked what was wrong? He *must* not have been feeling well, I was sure of it. Who would offer to take you to the movies then change their mind?

I believed with all of my heart this truth I had invented for him. I wanted to believe it, I had to believe it.

"Goodnight, ladies," he announced when we reached my door.

"Goodnight, George," I said politely. "I hope you feel, um... better," I told him.

He gave me a look of annoyance and his eyes got wide. He nodded, turned and walked away. My mother was sitting at the kitchen table and looked up at us, confused.

"What happened, girls?" she asked.

"Nothing, *Mama*. Something broke at the theater. I think it was the reel that got stuck or something." I said, hoping she could not detect my lie. "We're going to my room, *Mama*," I told her as my cousin and I walked hurriedly. I shut the door and leaned against it, as I sank to the floor and hugged my knees. I knew it was finally safe to cry.

"He doesn't want to marry me, I can feel it. Oh, Eleni! I have ruined everything!" I cried to my cousin.

"But what could you have ruined, Eleni?" she asked me. "You did nothing wrong." My cousin sat next to me on the floor, rubbed my shoulder and looked into my eyes.

"You know, you are not married yet, you can still call it off."

I stared straight ahead. No. I would not entertain it.

"Call it off? Eleni, this is a dream come true. I am so lucky," I started to tell her before she put her finger to my lips.

"My dear cousin, *he* is the lucky one. You are the dream. Don't ever forget it."

I looked at her and smiled.

"I mean it. I don't like his moods. There is something about him that makes me feel uncomfortable."

"No, Eleni. It's me. It's me. I can be better. I am going to try. You will see," I told her. We hugged and I cried some more. I felt weak after my emotional meltdown and my cousin helped me into my nightgown and brushed my hair. When I laid my head on my pillow, I did not even have the strength to dream.

Back on Ellas

Remembering my sadness that night makes me cringe and crunch my toes. For whatever reason, everything about that night felt wrong. Yet I insisted with everyone, including myself, that I still was sure about marrying George.

So here I sit, in the middle of the ocean on my way… My mind is a vast sea and there is a violent storm brewing. I can barely keep the waves from dragging me under. My mind thrashes and struggles to survive in these turbulent waters. I think I need to sleep, so that I can dream. In dreams, I can live in a happy, effortless place. Life seems too short for our struggles to be so great. I wonder if I will always be so… conflicted.

I never doubted the way Yianni felt about me. It was obvious, easy and natural as the earth beneath my feet on a warm summer day. I think it would be nice to write Yianni a letter, to tell him how I never realized the ocean was so big, that I hoped nothing would happen to this ship because we both know I cannot swim. He always made fun of me for my lack of swimming skills.

"*Tzitzika*, we live in a country surrounded by water and a thousand islands. How is it you have gotten this old and cannot even tread water?" I can hear his voice echoing in my mind, laughing at me.

But then I hear the angry, hurt voice. The other side of Yianni. The one I don't want to remember yet keeps repeating in my mind.

"Don't do this!"

Involuntarily, I raise my hands to my ears. I have done exactly what Yianni begged me not to do. I left Yianni, my mother, my family and all of my friends behind. My mother. The image of her consumes me. Her body collapsing in anguish as my *theo* tried to help her stand haunts me.

The Day After

The morning after George made us leave the movie theater, there was a knock at the front door. I rubbed my eyes, still puffy and tired from crying. What time was it? I wondered whether I'd slept the entire day. Where was my mother? Was she at work or in the garden? Disconnected, I stumbled towards the door. A man stood there with a bouquet of flowers.

"Delivery," he said.

"What?" I answered.

"Listen, I don't know why but this American gentleman came to my store insisting I deliver these flowers to you instead of him. Apparently this is how they do things in America." He handed me a small white card and the flowers and told me to have a good day.

I held the note: "Dear Eleni, I am sorry about the movies. Please forgive me? – George" A wide smile spread across my face. So he is not mad at me after all. I leapt around the house, singing as I placed the fresh flowers in a vase. So this is what they do in America? They send special delivery people to give their women flowers? I squealed with delight.

I put on a big smile the next few dates we had together. Laughing, smiling and always in my best dresses and mood. I ran out of funny stories though, and he did not have many of his own. In our short chaperoned outings we only covered the basics. I learned that he was one of six children and I explained how I was an only child. He told me a little bit about his life in America and I told him where I was raised and all about my family. I told him what I remembered from the war, and all about my father. Sometimes he looked at me like he had no idea what I was talking about when I mentioned the wars Greece endured. Did the news not reach America? It seemed a foreign, unimportant subject. It was the war and my mother's handling of it that helped to mold me. I was trying to show him who I was, where I came from, what my parents lived through and endured, how my father died. I knew part of the reason I was engaged to him was because of my father's wishes for my future. Without that, my uncles would not have pressured my mother to stay out of my decision.

Even though he was Greek, he didn't seem to hold a passionate love of his parent's native land. Sometimes I felt as if he was looking down on my country; it was not as nice as his comfortable American life. Of course these were unproven assumptions, but sometimes I felt it in a certain snobbery he exuded. I clung to moods and vibes, hoping for information.

My wedding was only a few days away. My mother, my aunts and my girlfriends buzzed around me. Angeliki came to visit with her new baby girl.

"Marriage is the best," she told me sitting on the edge of my bed. Her baby fussed and she went on talking to me as she effortlessly put her on her breast. "Of course we had the baby immediately… I am sure it would have been nice to have a little time first, but it is still wonderful. Manolis is really good to me," she said.

I smiled.

"I am so happy for you, Angeliki. It sounds like you have everything figured out. "

I was happy for her, but deep inside I was selfishly scared for myself.

Drunk

It was only a few days before our wedding. It was the first time I saw George drink alcohol. He was with my *Theo* Panayotis on the balcony and they were drunk. *Theo* drinks every day, so I was used to it. But George seemed like a completely different person. I stood below, looking at them for few moments. George was laughing and slapping his hands down on the table. He was involved in a long story. I had never seen him smile so much, or heard him laugh. Did age explain his usual seriousness or did sobriety? It appeared to be the latter, so, clearly I had my answer. I should understand that men were different when it is men among men versus men among women. They like their drinks and cigarettes, and women are supposed to accept it, no complaints. I wondered about George's friends in America and whether or not they were good company. Getting married, even moving to America was an easy choice. These were both things I wanted. But this mysterious, moody man who only laughed and smiled when he drank... that was not something I had anticipated.

I had always imagined my husband a sweet, loving man with a good family who loved me like their own sister and daughter, like Yianni's. I knew I had to try and control my thoughts better than this. I had to stop going back to him. But thoughts of Yianni appeared too often, no matter how hard I tried to stop them.

As my wedding day approached, I realized how often George's moods unnerved me. Sometimes it was nothing in particular he said or did, his presence alone unglued me. I did not dare tell anyone, especially my cousin Eleni. Something was out of place, strange and dangerous about him. I could not brush away the feeling that everything was about to go terribly wrong.

The Night Before

George gave me a gift the night before our wedding. I held the beautiful gold bracelet full of sparkling diamonds in the light and smiled thankfully.

"It was my mother's and her mother's. It is my mother's gift to you, to wear on our wedding day," George told me.

"Thank you so much. It is beautiful," I said. I could not escape the thought that this was intended for someone else. It was never supposed to be mine. It was sent here for another woman George would take for his wife. It was not bought or crafted for my wrist like the ring Yianni made me. I put the bracelet on and removed Yianni's ring. Somehow, they did not look right on the same arm. Wearing the bracelet felt like I had stolen something from someone. In a way, I had. But

I decided I would wear it on my wedding day graciously, to respect and honor his mother. Tomorrow would be the beginning of my future. I would peel back the layers of this mysterious man. Like an onion, piece by piece I decided I could get past the layers to his core, until I understood him, knew him and loved him like my own mother and father loved each other.

Before bed, I sat and stared in the mirror. I combed my hair slowly, remembering how this was the first glimpse of George I had, the mysterious American man, combing his hair slowly in my *thea's* mirror. Tomorrow I would be married to him. My mother entered my room and gently took over brushing. I relaxed at her touch. She looked at me in the mirror, her face tense and serious.

"Eleni-*mou*. I know I have not really told you any of this before, but there are some things you should know. Soon you will become a woman. You don't have to worry about it or anything. Just obey and listen to your husband and you will be fine. You will also have to cook, clean, do everything that I do. Do you understand? You must be ready for all of this. Do not be afraid, no matter what," she says.

"Of course, *Mama*. I know all of that," I said.

"You will be fine if you try your best. I know you will make George happy and me proud." She hugged me tight. I inhaled the smell of her; basil and earth.

Vasiliki's Perspective

My daughter, my only child. My blood. If I only could tell her how I was dying at the thought of her leaving, she wouldn't go. But how can I keep her, hold her close as an infant in my arms when she is a young woman at marrying age? My brother and brother in-law tell me she is lucky to have the opportunity for a better life. But she is my only baby and my sweet husband is gone. What other choice do I have but to leave Greece myself and follow her? After all the pregnancies, the pain of so many babies dying inside of me, she survived…. My Eleni. I know she will be alright because she is a survivor. Strong, like me. The only reassurance in letting her go is the knowledge that she will press on just as I have taught. America. Will this be the place to help us, heal us from our past and offer us salvation? I don't know, but I am hoping… Meanwhile, how do I tell my little moro (baby) good-bye? How does a mother let her child go so far away from them, at any age?

Preparations

The atmosphere was celebratory, sweet and small. Nobody from George's family had come from America. The only piece of them I had was this bracelet from my mother-in-law. I was also missing three friends, Athena, Vaso and of course Yianni. Athena and Vaso had not spoken to me or even looked at me since my engagement. They were too upset for their brother, and I was too guilty to look them in the eyes. I couldn't blame them. No one from his family was invited. My mother felt it was not appropriate given the circumstances of our families' intentions to commit their children to marriage. It was better to leave it alone and put it in the past. Why pour salt in the wounds my decision made?

Thea Maritsa and my cousin Eleni hovered over me, fixing my hair and makeup. My mother gathered the tray of wedding *koufeta* (sugar coated almonds) and placed the *stefana* (wedding crowns) on top of them. My mother taught me all about the symbolism. Honey dipped almonds covered in white sugar symbolize purity, fertility, endurance and sweetness. The *stefana* she placed on top are two crowns of flowers which are tied together with a single ribbon. They would be placed on our heads during the ceremony, where special prayers bind us together. The same almonds were given to guests, wrapped in lace or tulle in odd numbers. Odd numbers cannot be divided evenly. Therefore, the married couple shall remain undivided.

"Everything looks beautiful," I told my mother as she buttoned the back of my dress.

"*You* look beautiful," she said.

My dress was a combination of cream colored satin and lace. Underneath the satin and lace layers were four layers of tulle which gave the dress fullness. The sleeves were long, sheer and pleated. It was tight around the waist then flowed out in tiered rows. The lace was trimmed with sequins and pearls. It was gorgeous and I felt confident in it. I could hardly wait to be seen by everyone at the church.

Things started to move fast. Everyone swarmed about, gossiping, giggling and preparing to walk me down the street to the church. George waited for me there and according to tradition, he would formally ask my *Theo* Stathis for my hand before we walked down the aisle together.

My mother came toward me and locked my new family heirloom on my wrist. I put my arms by my side and the bracelet caught on to the lace. It pulled at my new dress viciously like a small angry animal, its teeth constantly nipping at me. It was almost as if the bracelet knew I was not the rightful owner. Each time my arm brushed near my dress, the lace tore. I wanted to take it off and not wear it at all but I knew George would look for it. I decided to hold my arm in an odd uncomfortable way instead of insulting my new family. My mother did not notice my struggle.

My mother placed my veil on my head. It flowed on the ground behind me at least six feet. My bridal costume was complete.

"Look in the mirror, *agapi-mou*," she said. It took a minute or two before I realized the face staring back at me was my own. My expression looked barren. My eyes were empty; somehow different than they were yesterday. My mother's arms embraced me from behind, and both of us looked at the mirror together. Her expression was sad. The only time I had ever seen a similar look was when my father died. The second closest was the night the German bombs shook our home in Athens and my *theo* told us Hitler's army was in Greece. She was about to lose me, yet she was trying her hardest to encourage me and my dreams.

"What is it, *Mama*?" I asked. Tears welled up in her beautiful eyes.

"I am just going to miss you too much, Eleni. I don't know how I will get along without you. I know George is a nice man, but I don't really know him or your new family. One conversation on the phone is not enough. I don't know anything about them. You will be so far away and I will be so worried all of the time," she said.

"Nobody could ever love or care for me the way you do, *Manoula-mou*. Please, don't worry," I reassured her.

"*Mama*, remember I will send for you soon. I will start working on it right away. You will be able to come to America, become a citizen and come and live with us. Everything will be fine. You'll see!" I said cheerfully, throwing my arms around her and kissing her on both cheeks over and over until she was smiling wide at me.

"Well…" she said. "You look beautiful today. You are the most beautiful bride I have ever seen… I love you so much." We were both on the verge of tears.

"Be careful-- you will ruin your makeup. Now let's go and have a wedding," she said.

"Yes, *Mama*," I agreed.

After we wiped our tears, my mother took my hand and we walked towards the church. I looked up at the cross which sat on the top of the church's dome, glowing in the sunset. Everything around me looked so beautiful.

Suddenly, I got a rush of fear that made me want to run. Yianni – where was he? I wondered. My hand became sweaty in my mothers. I glanced in every direction, looking for a sign that he was watching. I knew he was near. I wished for a moment that he would come bounding out of the shadows and kidnap me, removing me from this decision.

"What is it?" my mother whispered, squeezing my hand.

"Nothing, Mama," I lied, forcing a smile. My mother recognized the lie, but she didn't push. We were both in fragile states and one outburst of emotion could have made us crumble. My mother and I walked together toward my fate, to the large ornate double doors. So many people I loved were in there, waiting. *Breathe. Breathe.* I told myself as my pulse quickened.

Little did I know just how close Yianni was to where I walked. I knew he was there, I could feel it. He promised to be waiting until the church bells rang and I walked out a wife. Then, he promised to start the process of forgetting me. I took a deep breath and tried to calm my tortured heart. My *Theo* Stathis came out of the church to join us along with George. My groom smiled warmly at me. My heart sank because the instant I saw George's face, I thought of Yianni's.

"With your permission, may I please have Eleni's hand in marriage?" George asked.

"Yes, you may," *Theo* replied. He shook George's hand and kissed him on both cheeks. Then my *theo* looked at me, kissed me on both cheeks and whispered,

"Are you ready, *matia-mou*?"

"Yes *Theo*, I am." It was time to be happy and grateful for all I have received. I gave my mother and *theo* the widest smile I could then turned to George we locked arms. Then, we proceeded through the doors of the church.

A Cicada's Song

A cicada lives out the short season of its life long enough to fulfill one goal: sing in order to attract a mate. They then get to the business of reproduction. Their singing stops. Have they no need to put on their impressive show because they have gotten what they wanted? Yes. That is exactly what they do.

Near Yet Far

Yianni's Perspective:

It is 4:45 in the evening. I run as fast as my feet can carry me towards the church as the bells ring. She must be at the church by now, in white lace. Of course I have never seen her dress, I just imagine her in lace because I know she would look so beautiful in it. I cannot understand how she allowed her life to change overnight. How she made this choice so quickly, without really thinking through the cost of leaving home and everyone she loves. I don't think that her mind has processed the reality of losing me yet. What we were. What we are. What we were about to become. There has been no time! My heart races as I run. Memories of her appear at every corner as I race through our neighborhood streets. Her smile floods my mind.

I tuck myself against the wall on the far side of the church and wait. It will not be long now before she comes. Her rejection last week was the most painful thing that I have felt in my life. Although, somehow I felt she did not want to reject me. She was nervous about her marriage, I sensed it. Yet she was adamant whenever she made a decision.

Our kiss, and my foolishness for forcing it onto her, sickens me. But, the kiss was worth it. I still can feel the tingle on my lips. I remember how beautiful her green eyes glowed at me in the moonlight seconds after our kiss. How I long for so much more of her. It is not fair. I cannot begin to compete with what the American has to offer.

Darkness approaches. The sky has taken on a pinkish hue. Looking down, I see her. My angel in white lace. Pure and white, and as brilliant as the sun. I gasp at her beauty. She looks solemn in the procession with her mother. I want to run to her, take her away with me. I feel my body ready to shout her name and go to her side.

Something changes. She smiles. Wide and beautiful at her theo and he hands her over to him. She is happy! Tears burn my cheeks and I bury my eyes in my rough hands. These hands I have burned a thousand times when I crafted her ring. These scarred hands full of love, sweat and hope for our future were not enough. Nothing I did mattered. She wants a better life than I can ever provide. My heart breaks into a thousand pieces. Will I ever be able to fix it?

Ceremony

The sound of chanting and thick incense wafted through the air as we proceeded. I looked around and observed every ornate detail of the church, along with each and every icon. My eyes drawn, as always, to the icon of the *Panagia*, The Virgin Mary. I hide behind my heavy veil, face to face with the ultimate mother.

I missed my father. I wished he had been here to grant permission to George. I looked from side to side as I recognized all of my relatives and friends whom I loved so much. My eyes were filled with sad and happy tears simultaneously.

Row after row of eyes were fixated on me in silence. It was a little strange, being the center of attention like this. Orthodox ceremonies are beautiful and long. They consist of two parts: The Service of the Betrothal and the Ceremony of the Sacrament of Marriage. Everything in a Greek Orthodox ceremony has detailed symbolic meaning and I actually took time to pay special attention to my mother when she told me exactly how it was all going to happen today.

In the Betrothal, rings were exchanged. The priest placed them on the tips of our ring fingers then they were exchanged three times by my cousin Thanasi, our *koumbaro* (best man). The priest took our rings and held them up high, blessing them. Then he slid them all the way down our fingers. Our gold bands shone on our right hands, for it is the right hand of God that blesses, it was the right hand of God to which Christ ascended, and it is also to the right that those who will inherit the eternal life will ascend. The sign of the cross was made over our heads. George and I both bowed to the ground. As we became betrothed to one another, the church fell silent.

The priest spoke: "The weakness of one partner will be compensated by the strength of the other, the imperfections of one, by the perfection of the other. By themselves, the newly betrothed are incomplete, but together they are made perfect." I lifted my head up and George was staring at me with his large, dark eyes. I blushed behind my veil.

In the ceremony of the Sacrament of Marriage, prayers, the crowning, readings from the New Testament, Common Cup and circling the ceremonial table are the main parts. I wondered what my own parents wedding had been like.

Our wedding *stefana* (crowns) joined by a satin ribbon, symbolized the unity of us and presence of Christ who blessed and joined us. We were blessed by the priest in the name of the Father, and the Son, and the Holy Spirit. We were deemed King and Queen of our home. We committed to this rule with wisdom, justice, and integrity. The priest told us the woman is expected to obey the King and ruler of the home, the ultimate master. However, the King must give the Queen respect and they must grow their kingdom in unison and fairness.

Thanasi stepped behind us to exchange the crowns of flowers three times over our heads. Three times. Father, Son, Holy Spirit. I looked at my mother as the crowns were lifted and placed on our heads. I mouthed the words *I love you*, silently. My body tensed. My head ached. Words and prayers and ceremonial music swirled around me. The finality of what I was doing started to affect me. I could not swallow. More readings followed. One described the marriage at Cana of Galilee which was attended and blessed by Christ and for which he reserved his first miracle. He had converted the water into wine and gave it to the newlyweds. In remembrance of this blessing, we were each given a sip of wine from a shared cup. This is the "common cup" of life symbolizing the mutual sharing of joy and sorrow, the token of a life of harmony. I looked at George, who smiled kindly as the priest lead us in a ceremony of circling the table where the Gospel and the Cross sat three times. The first official steps as a married couple happened in these three circles. I was still shielded by my veil. George's eyes tried to burn through it, so see my face. The mystery under the veil seemed to undo him. Eleni came to my side to help lift the trail of my dress from catching on the table as we proceeded. The priest chanted and followed us around the table, holding on to the satin ribbon between our crowns that connected us. The hymns he sang were to remind us of the sacrificial love of marriage, a love that seeks not its own but is willing to sacrifice all for the other.

Once the ceremonial walk was completed, the priest removed the crowns and asked God to grant us a long, happy and fruitful life. He asked God to bless us with many children. He lifted the Gospel up into the air and separated our hands. He told us, "now only God can separate you from one another."

As the priest said these final words I smiled. Everything was beautiful. At the same time, I was nervous. I knew there are many marriages still being arranged like this, but I could not help but think of how much more it would mean if we were in love. If both of us had met, gotten to know each other for a while and grew our love, how beautiful would that be?

As I stood there dreaming, my veil was lifted by my new husband. I tried so hard to smile so wide that my neck tensed. I was a married woman and I had never once in my life been truly, madly deeply in love. I would love George. I hoped he would love me, too. He smiled as he leaned forward taking my hand in his.

I tried to feel the butterflies in my belly that I heard Angeliki talk about with Manolis. I knew I could be a loving wife and love my husband. I knew I could become the wife he would love and respect for a lifetime. Just like my mother and father. I wanted to tell George all of this. Maybe we did not fall in love before marriage, but my hope was that my *thea* was right. We would grow in love over time. We would fall in love later. Just the thought of witnessing love unfold excited me. Love that would grow. It gave me the happy feeling that I was doing the right thing after all.

The priest smiled. He told George he could kiss his bride. As George's face moved toward mine, I remembered Yianni in the rain, in my dream hit by the train, kissing me and begging me not to leave. *Give me some more time*, a simple request. *I love you.* Before I realized it, I had spoken the words I love you out loud. It was a whisper, but it was loud enough that George heard it. He smiled a crooked smile that seemed happy yet puzzled simultaneously. Then his lips were on mine. His kiss was hard and fast, and it was over before I could blink. Everyone clapped and I felt like I was about to lose my balance. An imaginary earthquake shook the church floor beneath me. Many emotions hit me at once. George noticed my unsteadiness and held my shoulder firmly.

No butterflies. No tingles. No *tzitzikas* buzzing in my head. The kiss from George was entirely different than my first kiss with Yianni. There was no tingling afterwards. No comparison. My hand in his felt normal, non-eventful. I touched my lip and smiled, looking at everyone in the church. My second kiss was nothing like the first, not even close. Everyone came up to congratulate us. My mother came first smiling and crying at the same time. Everything from that moment on was blurred and dream-like.

A thought came to my mind from another time, another place when I heard someone say: "Sometimes you can be married to one person and be in love with someone else. It does happen, you know." I couldn't remember where, but I had heard this before. Perhaps I had created it in my own mind.

Aftermath: Yianni's Perspective

I sat there on the ground, arms hugging my knees long after the doors closed and the ceremony began and ended. The only decision that makes sense at this point is to let her go and pursue whatever it is she wants. After all, is that not the point of love? To see the other one happy, even at your own expense? It seems I am living in a present that is not as I thought all this time, a past that is finished, and a future that will never be. Tell me then, what do I have left? Nothing.

"Yianni. Yianni. We have been looking everywhere for you!" My sister Vaso shakes my shoulder. I am not sure how long I have been sleeping here, with my head on my knees.

"Stop this, Yianni. I am afraid you are going to make yourself sick," Vaso tells me, holding me up and bringing me to my feet. I know that she will never forgive Eleni for what she has done to me, even though I have already forgiven her myself.

Reception

We danced, drank, a few dishes were broken and "Opa!" was shouted various times. Money was thrown when we danced, and I led the circular wedding song dance. Angeliki broke into the circle beside me and took my hand and kissed my cheek. "My little *Tzitzika*, I will miss you singing in the neighborhood. It will be so boring without you!" she told me as we danced. My life flashed before me as my family and friends spun in circles. I wove in and out of tables, through and under the arms of all those who I loved.

I decided to sit and eat something, though my appetite had vanished completely. Thanasi made a speech. He had barely started speaking and I was ready to burst into tears. I took a sip of champagne.

"George, we have not had much time to get to know each other, but you are a nice man. Take good care of her, or I will be knocking at your door in Boston." The room laughed. George frowned slightly.

"All kidding aside, our *Tzitzika* Eleni. We grew up together and shared so much. You are my sister. I am sure you will bring life and happiness for many years to your husband just like you have brought so much laughter and joy to all of your family and friends here in Greece. Many years together, my cousin! I love you." I raised my glass along with everyone else and drank the rest of the champagne in one gulp. I felt loved and happy, nervous and sad all at the same time. I was a wife. I was a child. I was afraid of my wedding night.

The thought of leaving this reception to go to the hotel alone with George startled me. I was so frightened, my palms grew sweaty. My entire body shook. I had the second kiss of my life at the church. Does the first one count since I did not even kiss Yianni back? My skin became white.

"Are you alright?" I felt my cousin Eleni's arm on mine. I smiled.

"Of course, a little hot from the dancing." I told her.

"I will get you some water," she said and ran off quickly. I knew once I was alone with George… I would have no idea, no experience. I did not know what to expect. No one has ever warned me or even explained sex to me. I struggle to breathe. I only heard small bits of Angeliki's details, most of which I did not understand. How much did she really understand, herself? After all, she got pregnant her first time. I looked at her across the room at her, dancing with Manolis happily. He whispered in her ear and she threw her head back, laughing. Long black hair flowed down her new, rotund, post-baby body. She hugged him as they danced. They looked so happy, so free. I could not help but wonder: *How do George and I look tonight, to this room full of people who know me so well? Do they sense how unnatural I feel, or have I played my part well enough? Surely, we do not look like Manolis and Angeliki.*

Fear gripped me hard. Hotel. Bed. The urge to escape the situation consumed every part of me. It must have been wedding night nerves. Everyone has them. Right? It is normal, I told myself. Angeliki warned me this might happen, that I might panic. The night went on. Soon, the guests departed with warm hugs and best wishes. Lastly, my mother kissed me and held me tight. "I will see you tomorrow, love," she told me. She had no words of advice for me. See you tomorrow when you and George come over to eat. That was it? I needed something more, advice, assurance, anything. My heart sank when she left and George took my hand. We walked upstairs to our room. George had been sniffling the entire evening. At first, I thought maybe he was emotional. I would be if my family and friends were not at my wedding. It became clear, however, that he only had a cold that seemed to worsen throughout the night. He looked and sounded terrible.

"You know, George there is a pharmacy right next to the restaurant downstairs. I am sure they have some medicine that will help you. I'll just clean myself up a bit."

"You're right. Wait right here, I will be right back," he said, kissing me on the forehead. He ran downstairs.

In my mind I heard German planes rip through the air. I see myself playing hopscotch, and I feel the panic. The fear that had gripped me then caused me to freeze. This time, the episode made me want to run. I could not stop pacing, I could not sit, my palms were sweaty, and I was shaking. Tonight I would have to give up my virginity to a man I hardly knew and did not understand. Yet, there I was, his wife. Fear told me to run. *You have five minutes, maybe ten at the most to be gone, I told myself.* I rushed downstairs, looking both ways for George. I still had my wedding dress on. It was long and bulky, which made it hard to navigate down the stairs.

"Good evening, Madam. Can I help you?" asked the hotel manager.

"No, thank you. Just getting some air," I lied. I headed through the back door into the street. It was late, and not many people were around. I ran down the street as my dress dragged on the cement and tore on every stone and tree along the way.

My head pounded. I had no idea where I was going, but I kept on running. I never slowed down. My bracelet became stuck to my dress. I pulled until it took a large piece of lace with it. I thought back to the two weeks of our engagement. How many times had I felt this quiet alarm going off in my head? Why did I ignore it?

My heart felt like it might come out of my chest and I felt dizzy. I did not even know where I was until I realized I had reached my *thea's* house. I thought I would hide there for a little while. I could collect my thoughts and breathe through this panic attack. I convinced myself that perhaps that is what it simply was, a panic attack and nothing more.

I thought everybody was probably at my mother's house by now, having a post wedding drink. The door was unlocked so I let myself in. I wiped the sweat from my forehead and looked up. To my shock, the room was full. My disheveled appearance surprised everyone. *Theo* Stathis came quickly to my side.

"What did he do to you? I will kill him! What happened? Are you hurt?" he asked.

"No. I just - It's just that. Well... I. Oh *Mama*! I don't want to be married anymore!" I cried. It was true. I did not want this anymore. Forget America.

"I want to forget this ever happened," I said, sobbing wildly. "Please, *Mama*!" I begged. She fixed everything. She could fix this, too. I knew she would.

She rushed to me, hugged me close and stroked my hair. She whispered the words I did not want to hear: "Eleni, you are a married woman now. You have to go with your husband," she said, kissing my face over and over. I felt betrayed. With burning eyes, I looked around the room for someone to oppose her opinion but everyone was silent.

If the circumstances were the same for another girl my age, I would like to think she might have reacted as badly as I did. I wanted to justify my behavior. But deep down inside, I knew I my behavior was inexcusable. What would everyone think of me now? Looking down, I could not believe how badly I had ruined my dress. I buried my head in my mother's shoulders and cried. It seemed like only a moment had passed when I heard George's voice.

"Eleni!" he bellowed, as he ran to me.

He was relieved immediately and examined me as if I had been harmed. He was disheveled himself. I felt a pang of guilt for putting him through that. He took me gently into his arms and hugged me.

I wanted to disappear. I wished an earthquake would open a crack right at my feet, just my size, and swallow me whole. I did not want this marriage, I did not want him. He sniffled and took a handkerchief from his pocket and blew his nose loudly.

Oh God. Help me. I prayed inside my head. Please, help me to be a good wife and do what makes my husband happy. Help me to LOVE him. Please, I can learn. I will. I will learn. I begged for some sort of relief or a sign, but I got nothing. Defeat is the only emotion I held in my heart. I looked up at George's face and said, "I am so sorry. I just got so – scared. I did not intend to insult you, or worry you like this."

"It's alright, Eleni. I was so confused when I found out you were gone. I could not have imagined what happened to you. I was worried."

Everyone in the room gave us encouraging smiles. We made our way around hugging and kissing everybody once more. I was embarrassed and reluctant. However, I promised myself that moment, there would be no turning back. I would be a good wife. I would do as my husband told me. I felt imprisoned, out of choices. Although this prison was my own creation, a prison I wanted to lock myself in. Until *death.*

My mother was sympathetic, but I could tell she was also disappointed. This was not a good first impression as a wife. By the time George and I entered the hotel room, I was exhausted. All I wanted was to get out of my dress and sleep.

Without having to explain anything, George looked at me with understanding. He took my chin in his hand and said: "Don't worry, Eleni. Take as much time as you need. We will take things slow, I promise. Let's just go to sleep tonight."

I had never seen this sweet, gentle side before. He was sincere. Through the thick haze of doubt and fear that surrounded came a positive thought: *maybe, just maybe, this would work after all.*

I tossed, turned and had too many startling dreams to remember or count. My jaw became sore from clenching my teeth. Meanwhile, George slept deeply and soundly beside me, snoring. At four o'clock the light of day started to seep into our window. I sat up and studied my husband. He looked so peaceful and content. I stared at his face and the shape of his body. He had broad shoulders and long legs. His legs were actually so long, the sheets barely covered his toes. I knew that I should not be afraid of him. But my mind could not tell my heart what to feel. As always, they lived in a state of constant disagreement.

First

The next morning, we went home to spend a few days with my mother before our honeymoon began. When we walked in, the house smelled of lamb and mint. My mother gave us her bedroom, which felt strange. But my bed was not big enough for the both of us. George continued to respect my fears. We spent the next few days laughing and eating with family and friends. We decided to go to the island of Santorini for one week for our honeymoon.

On the island, I took in the blue of the sea against the whitewashed buildings with pride. We saw the most beautiful sunrises and sunsets together. We went to the beach and enjoyed relaxing.

The third night, something in George's demeanor changed. He became more aggressive. He had a few drinks with dinner and his kisses got more urgent, more intense. I knew that this night would be different. War, death and my childhood all came crashing together as I crossed over from childhood to womanhood. I was ready, confident. I knew that I could be the woman he would want and always love.

As the experience happened before me, to me, I felt… waves crashing on the shore in a violent storm, salty air bitter in my mouth, air raid sirens and German planes flying overhead, the buzzing of *tzitzikas*, the smell of summer, hopscotch on the concrete, the faces of German and Italian soldiers, running in the olive groves to escape the train with my mother, falling off the merry-go-round, trapped underneath and how I felt when my baby doll was left behind. I thought I would lose her forever if a bomb came down and blew up our train. But it did not, and she still existed, packed in my trunk of things to bring to America. And suddenly I was thrown back into the present moment.

I could not describe it with any other word than *indifferent*. I felt everything and nothing at the same time. I looked to the ocean, wondering if I was feeling the way I should. But who is to say how one *should* feel? I wondered if my thoughts even mattered at this point. Love would grow. Time. All I needed was more of it. This is only the beginning.

George went back to America after Santorini and sent for me. My papers came fast and soon I was booked on the Greek ship *Ellas*, which would take me across the Atlantic Ocean to New Jersey. For nearly two weeks I would cross the Atlantic Ocean alone.

Back to the Present

Either it is my nerves or sea sickness but I am suddenly ill. I run for the small claustrophobic bathroom and throw up three times, bracing myself against the wall. I should go to my room and lie down. I wash my face, brush my teeth and put on some fresh clothes. It is only a matter of hours before we arrive now. George will be picking me up and we will drive to our new home together.

Arrival

It has taken two weeks at sea, but we are finally here. I am already thinking about how we will send for my mother. As the boat pulls into the port, I notice the water is brown and cloudy. We sit like pigs stuck in mud as the boat slowly anchors in the dirty water. Across the water is New York City. Then, I see it. The symbol of freedom for all who arrive in America. The great Statue of Liberty. She is a bland greenish grey color, but her height is impressive. She holds a large torch in her hand and something that looks like a book in the other.

"People can climb all the way up to the top and look out of the torch!" I heard someone say.

I stare in amazement but I also ponder: If her country is so wonderful, why doesn't she wear a big smile? I hear the voices of my friends behind me.

"Eleni! We have been looking everywhere for you!" Afrodite, Marina, and Christina take turns hugging and kissing me, petting me on the head as usual, like I was their little pet.

"Here is my address," said Christina.

"I am off to Canada, but perhaps you and your husband can visit or we can come to Boston one day!" she said excitedly.

It felt exciting to already be considering fun plans for me and George.

I stare at the mass of people below waiting on land, looking for George and his parents. I had only spoken to them on the phone once, after the wedding. I have no idea what they look like. From George's description of their personalities, however, I had my own images in my mind. I am on the high deck, where it is really hard to make out any faces. People look like ants from here. It certainly doesn't help that all men seem to be wearing the same exact black and grey hats. I should get down lower, but the crowds are hard to navigate. I have always needed glasses, to take the slight blur out of everything. They would really come in handy now, I think to myself. I don't even know where I have buried them in my luggage since I never use them. I scan the crowd until I finally see George's figure approaching the dock, waving and jumping up and down. I smile, excitedly waving back. I wonder where his parents are, and why he has come alone. I was sure he would have brought them along to greet me. Suddenly, I hear my American name. I forgot to listen for it for a while. I recognized the voice, it is George's.

"H-E-L-E-N!" he beckons again, in an annoyed manner.

His irritated tone sends a ripple of panic through my body. To my horror, the person I had been waving to was not my husband. I see the three of them below, George and his parents. They are standing together waving. I am embarrassed and wondered if they noticed I did not know my own husband. I wave back and smile. The captain announces that the doors will be opening and we must make our way towards the exit doors. I take a deep breath and head down, following the masses to the exit. America - I have arrived. The sky is dark grey. It looks as if it will rain any moment.

George and his parents greet me immediately with warm hugs and kisses. My mother-in-law wipes back a hair from my face and holds her hand on my cheek. We lock eyes for a moment and she smiles. I have sea legs. As I follow them to the car, the ground beneath me sways from side to side. My mother-in-law's name is Sofia. It means wisdom in Greek. It suits her. She is quiet, sweet, short and petite. At a closer look, her eyes seem tired and overworked, almost sad. Alexandros, George's father, is stern and serious. George resembles him most. We drive to a town called Methuen, north of Boston. We are going to live with his parents until we can get a home of our own. Hopefully it won't be long. George promised me on our honeymoon that it would be a year or less. George greeted me with a brief kiss, a feather light peck. He escorts me to his vehicle, which is impeccably clean. It is beautiful. The paint is so shiny and flawless, the inside is spotless as well. Everything is simply pristine! This made me smile. I love when things are neat and in order. He was just as handsome as I remembered. I put my hand on his and squeezed it. He smiled. I stretched out my feet before me in the passenger seat.

It is late fall in Massachusetts. Winter is coming soon. A chill creeps into my bones which is so raw it is utterly painful.

"You will toughen up to the cold, Helen. Don't worry," George says. I cringe on the inside.

"Thanks," I say, still clenching my teeth as to not let them chatter.

"How was your trip?" his mother, Sofia asked me. "Did you have smooth or rough seas?" my father in law, Alexandros, chimed in.

"Everything was fine, very nice ride and I met some nice people," I tell them.

George's face turned dark and he frowned slightly. "You are a married woman now, Helen. You shouldn't have spoken to so many people. But, I guess no harm was done, you will not really have to be alone like that, from now on anyways," he said as he made an effort to lighten his tone with every word. My face turned red and hot instantly.

I did not reply but looked out the window, trying to hide my embarrassment from the three of them. He forced a smile like he was joking with me, looking back at his parents. But there was something strange and jealous in his voice. Did he think I should not have spoken to a soul for weeks? Maybe he is joking. After all, he has a dry sense of humor.

It takes almost four hours to reach the long driveway of my new home. My legs grew tired from being in the same position and I put my feet up on the dashboard. George glared at me with big eyes. I immediately put them back down, apologizing.

When we arrive, there is more green grass and flat land than I had ever seen. The houses are so big, they look like mansions. I have never seen a single family home with three floors. But some of the homes are strange, squat in stature and made of wood.

"What are these, *parangas* (shacks)?" I asked, innocently. The only wood houses I knew of were makeshift homes built by gypsies on the outskirts Athens. I have seen them before. Simultaneously, George and his parents burst out laughing. I felt myself blush.

"This is how we build homes here, Helen. Not out of stone but wood," George said.

"Are they strong enough? What if there is an earthquake?" I asked.

"We don't get those here," George says.

Well, that is a good thing, I think to myself.

He parks the car and opens my door.

"Welcome home," he says with a warm smile. As I exit the car, his sisters and brothers walk toward me.

One of his sisters hops in front of the rest and smiles warmly. She grabs me by the shoulders and squeezes me tight.

"I am Catherine!" she says excitedly. A little girl peeks out from behind her leg. "This is my daughter, Maria." I bow down to her level and put out my arms to her. She momentarily hesitates then fills my arms with sweet little girl warmth.

My heart melts. George smiles. "She likes you," he says. "So, before I was interrupted..." he says glancing at Catherine. "I wanted to introduce you to everyone myself." Catherine looks away rolling her eyes at George.

"And this is Chris, my eldest but not smartest brother." Chris is a little thick in the belly and I am guessing he is in his late thirties. His eyes are very sweet.

"Thanks for the compliments as usual, George." He says in a tone more annoyed than joking. He takes my hand to shake it then kisses each cheek and gives me a nice hug. "My brother is lucky to have married you," he says. "Beautiful," he says, looking at his brother. I smile.

"This is Penny," George says. She is the second oldest girl. Catherine is the oldest I gather as she appears to be the only one with a child.

"Nice to meet you," Penny says and shakes my hand. I notice she has small hands and thin fingers and they feel like a child's hand in mine. She is short and petite like her mother Sofia. She is shy and does not hug or move forward to kiss me and she backs away after our handshake.

"Next, is John or baby brother," says George. I guess by looking at him that he is somewhere in his mid-twenties.

There are two more sisters I learn their names are Tina and Olga. Tina is very sweet but not as outgoing as Catherine. She is rather tall and she looks a lot like George.

My last introduction is to Olga. She is tall and thin as well with a long, crooked nose. Her handshake is cold like ice. I can almost sense immediately from her demeanor that she is not a warm person.

After introductions on the front porch, my new family leads me into the house carrying my things. Immediately as the door opens, I smell the most wonderful smell. My new sisters have prepared a delicious dinner of lamb and lemon potatoes, salad and fresh baked bread. I eat it like I have never eaten before. I did not realized how famished I was until I took the first bite. This is a meal my mother would have cooked and it comforted me.

Casual conversation flowed. Everyone seemed so kind and sweet – that is, with the exception of Olga. Even Tina and Penny, who seemed shy at first, took part in the conversation. They seemed like interesting women who I would like to get to know.

Olga. I could not comprehend why she seemed so angry and bitter. By the time dinner ended, I realized that if I was smart, my first priority in my new life is to try and steer clear of her whenever possible. George's other sister Catherine, I immediately decided, will become a great friend. She and her daughter Maria remind me of the relationship I have with my mother.

Everyone is married with the exception of Olga. She still lives with her parents. *Lucky me*, I think to myself. It is not going to be easy to avoid her. I take a deep breath as I glance out of the kitchen window. The sun is starting to go down for the night. The closest neighbor is so far down the road, it is not visible from my new home. I am really in the country now. This farm land looks more desolate than my mother's village in the dead of winter. There is not a soul walking down the street, as I am used to in the city in the evening. I feel as if I have landed on a different planet. But it is a promising planet, I remind myself. One that will offer a great life for my mother and I and the children I have one day. I know it will take time for this to feel like home, which is fine; I certainly have lots of it.

Then why do I have such a painful sadness that will not let up inside? *He is not the one.* There it is again, the annoying voice that speaks to me. But he *is one.* He is not somebody I married because we fell passionately in love. Deep inside, I know the truth: I have ignored my heart's desire for a chance at a better life. At first, it sounds depressing. But maybe trading a better life in a better place with endless opportunity is a fair trade to make. "True love."

I take a shallow breathe and my heart skips a beat. I am excited and nervous for this new part of my life. I remember what my *Thea* Maritsa told me before I left: "You will learn to love him. Love in marriage comes with the passage of time."

Promising myself to do my best, I take a deep breath and pray that her wisdom proves true. Right now, it is all I have, all I can hope for.

That night, as I lay in my new bed trying to absorb everything that has happened to me these past few months, I heard my father-in-law speaking to George downstairs.

"She is a baby, not a woman. What were you thinking, George? Tell me. What are you going to do with her?"

I close my eyes and do the sign of the cross over my body. I go deep into prayer, to God first then I unconsciously switch and speak directly to my father.

"Papa, I made it. Are you proud? I made it… to America."

A sudden lump forms in my throat as tears begin to fall down my cheeks. I have never felt so alone or afraid in my life. Then I heard George's answer to his father's question: "I don't know."

THE END

Greek Word Glossary

Agapi – love

Athina - Athens

Kastana – chestnuts

Chrystogena - Christmas

Diavolos – devil

Ekklesia - church

Ellas – Greece

Ena, thio, tria – one, two, three

Horyo – village

Iconostasis – wall of icons

Icon – image

Kafineon – café

Kalamatianos – type of Greek line dance

Kalokeri – summer

Kardia – heart

Koliva – wheat offering for departed persons

Koufeta – sugar coated almonds

Koukla – doll

Koumbaro – best man

Krifo Scholios – secret schools who taught Christianity during Greece's Ottoman occupation

Kyrie eleison – Lord have mercy

Manoula, Mama – mother, mom

Moro – baby

Mou – my

Mati – evil eye

Matia - eye

Onoma – name

O Theos – God

Ouzo – licorice liquor

Oxi – no

Panagia – Virgin Mary

Papa - father

Paranga – shack

Plateia – town square

Sika - fig

Stefana – wedding crowns

Thea – aunt

Theo – uncle

Tzitzika - cicada

Vasiliko – sweet basil

Yiasou – hello/goodbye

Yiayia – grandmother

Yifti – gypsy

Xenos – foreigner, outsider

Eleni's Family Tree

Eleni's Immediate Family Members:

Eleni - Main character

Vasiliki – Eleni's mother

Kosta – Eleni's father

Thea Maritsa – Vasiliki's sister

Theo Stathis – Vasiliki's brother in-law married to her sister Maritsa

Cousin Adonis – Thea Maritsa and Theo Stathis's son, oldest

Cousin Yiorgos – Thea Maritsa and Theo Stathis's son, middle child

Cousin Vangeli – Thea Maritsa and Theo Stathis's son, youngest (just a baby when WWII began)

Thea Maria – Kosta's sister in law married to his brother Panayotis

Theo Panayotis – Kosta's brother married to Thea Maria

Cousin Eleni – Thea Maria and Theo Panayoti's daughter, a few years younger than Eleni the main character

Cousin Thanasi – Thea Maria and Theo Panayoti's son, best man in Eleni's wedding, a few years older than Eleni the main character

Cousin Aggelos – Injured in the massacre at Kalavirta, son of Aggelos and Soula

Cousin Michali – Killed in the massacre at Kalavirta, married to Soula, oldest brother of Thanasi and Eleni

Cousin Soula – Married to Michalli who was killed though her son Aggelos survived

Eleni's in-laws:

George – Eleni's husband

Helen – Name George gave Eleni for her new life in America

Sofia – George's mother, Eleni's mother-in-law

Alexandros – George's father, Eleni's father-in-law

Chris, Penny, Catherine, John, Olga, Tina – George's siblings

Eleni's Friends and other Characters:

Yianni – Eleni's childhood friend and first love

Angeliki – Eleni's girlfriend who got pregnant and married Mannolis

Voula – The neighbor who went mad when her children and husband died of starvation in Athens

The Friedberg's - German neighbors who had become Greek citizens then sided with the German's for their own safety.

Diavolos – troubled kid in Eleni's neighborhood who picked on her and everyone else.

Thalia and Alessio – Greek girl and Italian solider who fell in love, married and escaped to Italy

Athena – Eleni's childhood friend, also one of Yianni's sisters

Vaso – Eleni's childhood friend, also one of Yianni's sisters

Afrodite, Christina, Marina - Friends Eleni met on the boat ride to America

Discussion Questions

Eleni had to make a choice whether or not to marry a man twice her age at sixteen years old. What are your feelings about her choice? What would you have done in her place? Do you think she was too young to make such a decision?

Do you think Eleni's uncles influenced her choice by expressing how much her father would have wanted this better life for her? What do you think would have happened if she said no to George's proposal? Do you believe she really had a choice?

Many times the question of faith arises for Eleni. Do you think her faith is as strong as her mother's?

How do you feel about Yianni, her childhood love? Does she really love him or is the guilt of hurting someone she cares so much about the main cause of her anxiety?

Eleni's mother is a strong woman. How do you think she came to terms with letting her daughter go? Would you be able to do the same for your only child if you were in her shoes?

How do you think war and the loss of her father affected Eleni? If her father were alive, do you think things would have gone differently?

What do you think of George? Are there warning signs that Eleni may have trouble ahead? Why do you believe George behaves the way he does?

Do you feel that Eleni truly believes over time she will learn to love George? Do you think it is possible to marry first, fall in love later?

What do you think Eleni's life will entail once she arrives in America? Will she have everything she ever wanted? Do you feel George will be a good husband?

Cicada's Consequence

Book #2 of the Cicada Series Preview:

This strange new land is odd and cold physically and psychologically. It does not take long for me to come to terms with the truth of what I have done: For a moment of fickleness; a poor judgment of love, I will pay for a lifetime. This price I pay in installments, piece by piece, year after year. My consequence is violence. My killer and I stand face to face. His large, long fingers try to squeeze the life from me. I stare deep into his eyes as my vision begins to blur. Deep brown chocolate eyes that do not contain an ounce of sweetness. My life flashes before me. My mother and I survived war. If we can outwit a war, we can survive this man. I cannot die this way. I cannot give up. But his grip is so tight. The room gets fuzzy and I strain to breathe. My hands make their last desperate attempt to pry his fingers off me, clawing at his skin with my nails to no avail. The stench of alcohol fills my nostrils and thoughts flash to my beautiful children's faces. Blackness covers my eyes like a blanket, as my body goes numb. So, this is what it feels like to die…

Author Bio

Nitsa Olivadoti comes from a strong artistic and cultural background. She graduated from Bridgewater State University in 2000 with a major in Fine Arts and a concentration in painting. Her visual work has been displayed in student shows, online and local galleries and cultural festivals.

Born of a Greek mother and Swedish father, she had wanted to write her maternal grandmother's story since she was nine years old. It was only a matter of time. At thirty-one, with the encouragement and inspiration from her grandmother, she started the journey. Nitsa completed extensive research in European history, particularly on Greece during World War II, in order to support her grandmother's recollection of past events. Nitsa resides near Boston, Massachusetts with her husband and two children.

Nitsa can be contacted at: cicadaseries@gmail.com or visit her website for more information: www.cicadaseries.com

Editor Bio

Elaina Schlumper is an experienced Communications Professional with a strong background in editing, writing and research. Prior to working on Cicada's Choice, she worked within the Publishing, Media and Education Industries for over 12 years.

Elaina graduated from Regis College (Weston, Mass.) in 2000 with a Bachelor of Arts in Psychology and a minor in Communications. She enjoys dancing (which she has done for over 30 years) as well as reading and spending time with her husband and their two children. Elaina can be contacted at: elainaschlumper@yahoo.com.

22066227R00148

Made in the USA
Lexington, KY
10 April 2013